W9-BLL-153

SHIPWRECK SEASON

BY DONNA HILL

U.S.
LIFE SAVING SERVICE
DISTRICT №2
PERKINS HOLLOW STATION
SURFMAN
№ 6

CLARION BOOKS/NEW YORK

Research for *Shipwreck Season* was partially funded by
The Dr. Lolabel Hall Scholarship from the New York State
Division of The Delta Kappa Gamma Society International

Clarion Books
a Houghton Mifflin Company imprint
215 Park Avenue South, New York, NY 10003
Text copyright © 1998 by Donna Hill

The text is set in 12/15-point Electra

Printed in the USA.

Library of Congress Cataloging-in-Publication Data

Hill, Donna, 1921-
Shipwreck season / by Donna Hill.
p.   cm.
Summary: In 1880, forced to work with his uncle at a lifeguard station
on Cape Cod, sixteen-year-old Daniel finds himself maturing as he
encounters unexpected comradeship, challenges, and danger.
ISBN 0-395-86614-6
[1. Lifesaving—Fiction. 2. Cape Cod (Mass.)—Fiction.] I. Title.
PZ7.H549Su   1998
[Fic]—dc21
97-16739
CIP   AC

QUM 10 9 8 7 6 5

For Bob, Darrell, and Marvin

SHIPWRECK SEASON

ONE

"I can't do that, Bessie. I'm surprised you'd ask."

Coming in the front door, Daniel heard his uncle speaking to his mother in the drawing room. Although his uncle seldom raised his voice, somehow it was always commanding and annoying.

Daniel made a face. To Daniel, his uncle was a crude man in thick boots and rough clothes smelling of seaweed, but to Daniel's mother, he was a hero.

What was the man doing in Boston just at the start of the lifesaving season? He ought to be at his station on Cape Cod, browbeating his crew of surfmen.

Daniel could not hear his mother's soft reply. What did she want from his uncle? Daniel dropped his bag of rowing togs and crept toward the drawing-room doors.

"Bessie, not even soldiers at war risk more than my men do, rowing out to a wreck in the teeth of a storm. You don't know how hard it is, even for trained surfmen, to see a thing like last year, when a mariner we were trying to save lost his hold in the rigging and fell screaming into the sea."

"Oh, Elisha, that's horrifying, but—"

"We can't even save ourselves sometimes. Remember a few years ago, when we lost a man from our crew in a surfboat accident?"

"Yes, of course. His name was Charlie something, wasn't it? He was about to be married. It was so tragic. But Elisha, what am I to do if you can't help me?" She sighed.

Such a delicate and pretty woman had very effective sighs, as Daniel knew. She had been able to get her way in everything with Daniel's father. Daniel himself, though he loved her, had developed a certain immunity to those sighs.

"Can't you stay a few days so we can talk it over?" she asked.

"Wish I could, but our district superintendent is coming for inspection. I'll have to take the train back tomorrow."

"Oh, I do so dislike trains! They make everything go at such a pace. In the old days when Nigel and I took Daniel to the Cape for the summer, it was a lovely, leisurely trip by packet boat."

Daniel's uncle laughed. "And then a long rattling ride by coach."

"But people didn't go anywhere unless they meant to stay a while."

"Bessie, this is 1880. We have to change with the times."

Daniel's mother sighed again. "What am I to do, then, Elisha? Daniel has done so poorly in his studies that the school will not have him back this fall."

Daniel gasped. So this was about him!

His mother went on. "The headmaster thinks Daniel should find employment. If he can learn responsibility and catch up with his schoolwork, they may let him return next year."

A chair creaked as Daniel's uncle got up. The floor squealed as the man's great boots tramped the carpet. "If he hasn't been studying, what's the boy been doing?"

"He's joined some sort of athletic club with young men of the best families, he says, but it seems to me that all they do is amuse themselves."

Daniel snorted. His friends were good fellows, every one, especially Arthur. Arthur was not only a true friend and a great athlete, but he had important plans for his future. He was not just amusing himself.

"Just now they're training for a regatta," his mother was saying. "Last winter they took lessons from a boxing master. Last spring it was cycling. Daniel says his machine is called an ordinary, but I say it's a monster—huge front wheel, tiny back wheel. I don't see how the thing stays upright."

Daniel's uncle was laughing again. "Surely you approve of his building a strong body?"

"It's not that. It's all the rest."

"You mean his schoolwork."

There was a pause.

"That's all, isn't it, Bessie?"

"Oh, Elisha, from what he's let slip, I'm afraid those friends of his have led him to value the wrong things."

Daniel was not aware that he had let anything slip.

"He says, 'Drink like a gentleman' and 'A gambling debt is a debt of honor.'"

"I see."

"I'm afraid I've spoiled him since his father died. I haven't known how to make a man of him. Now I feel he's at a crossroads and I can't help him. He won't listen to anything I say. Oh, Elisha, I do so despair for his future."

Daniel was astonished. He knew that his mother was annoyed with him, but not that she was so seriously worried.

"What about a job in Nigel's firm?"

"That wouldn't do, Elisha. I must get him out of Boston, away from those friends of his. He needs strong supervision by men of good character. Naturally I thought of Cape Cod."

"The fishing season ends soon, but he might find work in Fleetport. The blacksmith is a good man. So is the cooper."

Daniel was outraged. Shoe horses? Make barrels?

"Oh, Elisha, I was so hoping he could be with you and your men."

Daniel's face went hot. How much worse than shoeing horses it would be at the lifesavers' station, taking

4

orders from his uncle, among the coarse, dull surfmen of his crew!

"I couldn't ask for a more wholesome environment for him," Daniel's mother added. "Or better examples of manhood."

Daniel could hardly believe what he was hearing.

"I guess I don't understand why you can't take him," she went on. "You wouldn't have to put him in actual danger."

"Danger aside, Bessie, I just can't do it."

"But why? You are the keeper, the captain. The surfmen and the station are entirely under your command."

"But I don't make the rules. The rules come from the General Superintendent in Washington. And they're strict, believe me. It's not like the old days when lifesavers were volunteers. Now they have to sign articles of enlistment and meet tough standards of health, strength, skill with boats, and knowledge of the coast. It's no job for a city boy."

Daniel listened with indignation. After all, he was an athlete, an oarsman, a swimmer. He could do anything a surfman could do, and face any danger.

"I couldn't take Daniel in any case. I already have a full crew. Not only that, keepers are discouraged from enlisting their kin."

"But I don't want him to enlist. He could never hope to be a surfman! Couldn't you just have him there? I'd gladly pay for his keep."

"We're not a nursery, you know."

"I'd want him to work. It's not as though he had nothing to offer. He's sixteen now, big and strong, more like his father every day, same black hair, fair complexion. He shaves now, too, although only he can see any fuzz." His mother laughed nervously, as though aware she had begun to babble. "Couldn't he help with ordinary chores? Shine equipment or something? Release your men for more important duties?"

Hearing his mother's lovely, persuasive voice, Daniel began to feel anxious.

"If only he could grow up to be a man like you, Elisha. I would ask nothing more of this life."

Of everything Daniel had heard his mother say, that was the worst.

"Daniel!" Mrs. O'Till, their housekeeper and resident martinet, was at his elbow, glaring at him. Though short, plump, and the age of a grandmother, she had the rosy face and vigor of a girl. At times, Daniel still found her intimidating, but he tried not to let her know it.

"I'll thank you not to sneak up on me," he said.

"Eavesdropping! Shame on you."

"I was just passing by."

"Tell that to the marines."

Daniel had to laugh. He liked Mrs. O'Till in spite of himself. She was more like a family member than a housekeeper.

"Daniel?" his mother called. "Come look who's here!"

Daniel went into the drawing room reluctantly.

"Isn't it good to see Uncle Elisha again?" his mother asked. "Isn't he more like your grandfather than ever?"

Daniel felt a rush of sympathy for his mother, looking for her lost husband in her son, her lost father in her brother. She had on a becoming dress with a fashionable bustle, and she looked delicate, young, and pretty, with her auburn hair piled up and ringlets at her ears. Daniel was pleased to see her happy for once, even though at the moment he was annoyed with her. He kissed her before offering his hand to his uncle.

Because Daniel had grown taller since their last meeting, he expected his uncle to seem shorter, but the man towered over him. His uncle's great shoulders, bulging in his seaman's jacket, were still amazing. Although he was not much older than Daniel's mother, his leathery skin, thick sideburns, and coarse unruly hair did remind Daniel of the grandfather he had known and loved long ago. That did not soften him toward his uncle.

"Good to see you, my boy," his uncle said. He took Daniel's hand in a gentle clasp as though greeting a child, but his other hand squeezed Daniel's biceps. Testing my muscles, Daniel thought indignantly, but he was proud that he would not be found soft.

Daniel's uncle had on a fresh shirt and his nails were scrubbed clean. But there was nothing Uncle Elisha could do about what he was, a dull brute of a man with nothing in his life but hard work. How could Daniel's mother want her son to be like that?

Daniel was anxious to know what they would do

about him, but he could not offer his own opinions without revealing that he had been listening at the door. All he could do was wait until they were ready to tell him.

TWO

THE TRAIN ROCKED AND SHRIEKED. The four hours from Boston to Fleetport on the Old Colony Railroad seemed forever. Cinders and vile smoke blew in through cracks around the window and into Daniel's hair and teeth. He had tried to doze in the jolting seat, but he was too upset to relax.

When first aboard, he'd been so distressed that he had wolfed down all the food Mrs. O'Till had provided, chicken, muffins, and cherry tarts, without enjoying any of it. Now he was hungry again, and his feelings were painfully confused. He was sorry to have been angry with his mother. He had tried every argument and every promise he could think of to keep her from sending him away, but in vain.

"On my honor, I will make up all my schoolwork."

"Daniel, you have had your chance."

"But it's too much punishment for failing in school."

9

"It's not punishment. Don't you understand? It's to help you learn what's important in life."

Daniel had not even been allowed to wait for the regatta.

"It's not fair. Why do I have to let the crew down?"

"Surely the club has other oarsmen."

"Not as good as I am!"

"Daniel, I am sorry for that, but your uncle is doing a lot for you. You must get there when it's best for him."

Daniel's feelings toward his mother had mellowed. She was simply being a mother. But she failed to see that her job was finished; he was grown up now, with his own interests and naturally resentful of interference. He understood her, but he still raged against his uncle. At bottom he knew that wasn't right, either, because the man had not even wanted him. Daniel hardly knew what to do with his frustration.

Arthur, their coxswain, hated to lose him from the crew, but good fellow that he was, he had tried to cheer Daniel up.

"It might be rather a lark, you know."

Daniel didn't think so, and now here he was with aching head, stiff neck, and sooty clothes, already missing the good times with his friends, stuck on this nightmare of a train, doomed to eight months of misery.

It seemed they stopped at every village on the Cape. They chugged into hill country in view of the bay. At Yarmouth, an old codger in a seaman's jersey came aboard and stood beside Daniel until he took his Gladstone off the seat to make space for him.

The man settled his bag on his knee and pulled off his cap, revealing a sun-browned pate with a fringe of white hair. "Where you headed, young feller?"

Daniel pretended to see something of interest glide by.

"You from up Boston way? Shouldn't wonder, from the look of you. Never been to Boston, myself. Never had a mind to. Been to Singapore, though. And New Zealand. Seen islands in the South Seas nobody ever heard tell of. Been around the world more times than I can think on, in whalers and merchant ships both. Bet you expect me to say I was a sea captain."

Daniel turned to the man to say he didn't want to talk, that he had a headache, which was true enough, but the old man's eyes were so bright and eager that he answered in spite of himself. "Were you a sea captain?"

"Nope. Second mate. You'll meet many a captain on the Cape but nary a second mate." He chortled. "It takes special talent to be a second mate. The captain gives the orders and the first mate hands them on, but the second mate sees them carried out. He's got to have a mighty stock of cuss words." He chuckled so hard that spittle blew out of his mouth.

Daniel turned away again, but the old man went on.

"Been a farmer, too, in my day. The Old Colony was pretty tolerable farm country once, corn and wheat as far down Cape as Truro. Down means north on the Cape. South means up. Bet you didn't know that, young feller."

"Yes, I did. I used to spend every summer in Fleetport."

11

"Fleetport was a mighty busy place in the old days. A mighty port for mackerel fishing, salt plants everywhere. Whaling, too—had eighty sail of vessels once. But the last whaler went out ten year ago. Going to visit kin, be you? . . . I say, going to visit kin?"

"My uncle."

"By what name? Might be I know him."

"Alder."

"Any kin of the keeper at Perkins Hollow Station?"

"He is the keeper."

"Well, I'll be jiggered! Know him I do and no mistake. That's the finest man I ever expect to meet this life. Got a gold medal for heroism, he did. Bet you didn't know that. He don't brag on it. Let me shake your hand! Proud to know anybody by the name of Alder."

The old man had a crushing grip.

"I'm not an Alder," Daniel said, pulling free with difficulty. "I'm a Stafford. The captain is my mother's brother."

"That would be Bessie, would it? Went off to Boston with a husband? I knowed her, too, from the time she was no taller than my boots. Knowed your grandparents. Never a better family in these parts."

Now there was no stopping the old man. He went on, first about the pirate Black Sam Bellamy whose vessel was sunk offshore near Perkins Hollow Station, then about the first vessel wrecked on the Cape, the *Sparrowhawk*, not much bigger than a surfboat, that carried forty passengers from England. He was starting

12

on the proper way to drain cranberry bogs when the conductor called out Eastham.

The old seaman popped his cap on his head and took up his bag. "Listen, young Alder. Don't let nobody pull your leg. Don't ask nobody on the Cape if he lived here all his life, or you'll get, 'Not yet.' Don't ask if the weather's going to clear up, or you'll get, 'Always has.'"

Cackling, he offered his hand, but Daniel managed to avoid his bruising grip.

"Tell your uncle that Barnaby Duff sends high regards."

The train clattered on through a woods where pine trees grew to the edge of the tracks. A village appeared, with tall masts rocking beside wharves and docks.

The conductor called, "Fleetport!"

With a great sigh, Daniel gathered his belongings.

THREE

DANIEL STEPPED OFF THE CHUFFING train and saw his Uncle Elisha on the platform, towering above the crowd. Men touched their caps to his uncle; women smiled up at him. Among these people the man was outstanding, even rather handsome. Here his seaman's jacket looked just right on his great shoulders.

His uncle embraced him. "Welcome, my boy!" He looked at Daniel's Gladstone. "Is this all you brought?"

"No. We sent my trunk ahead."

Leading Daniel into the depot, his Uncle Elisha asked, "How was your trip?"

"Some old codger yammered at me from Yarmouth to Eastham. Old man must have been sixty. Barnaby somebody."

His uncle laughed. "Barnaby Duff. He's past ninety. Still plays a mean fiddle, though, and does a mean hornpipe."

It was a small depot, with benches, a stove with a pile of wood beside it, a huge wall clock, and a board of notices.

The agent came out from behind his ticket window, dragging Daniel's trunk. "Here's his baggage, Captain."

Daniel's uncle shook his head. "Sorry, my boy, but we don't have room for anything this size. We'll take out what you need and send the trunk back. Open it, please."

"But I need everything in here."

"Open it or it goes back as is." His uncle turned to the agent. "Seth!"

"Wait!" Daniel said. "I'll open it."

The tray was filled with neckties, gloves, scarfs, hose, handkerchiefs, and toilet articles. Mrs. O'Till had raised objections, but Daniel had made sure she left nothing out.

Daniel's uncle said, "Take handkerchiefs, socks, one necktie, and your toilet articles." He removed something from under a pile of handkerchiefs. "Playing cards?"

"The men get to relax once in a while, don't they?"

"Cards are against regulations. Lift the tray, please."

When Daniel did so, his uncle said, "Leave the suits and varnished shoes. Take two linen shirts, the night-shirts, slippers, and your books. Your mother said you're to work on Latin, history, and mathematics."

Fuming, Daniel obeyed.

"What have we here?" His uncle held up two bottles that Daniel had slipped in after Mrs. O'Till had finished packing.

"Sherry. From my father's cellar."

"Alcohol is not allowed at the station."

"Why are you treating me like a child!"

"This is not about you. It's about regulations."

His uncle carried the bottles to the ticket agent. "Take these for Thanksgiving, Seth."

"No rule against it at our house." The agent grinned.

Daniel's uncle went on. "You may keep your hat and gloves for church, Daniel. Pack your Gladstone with what I've said you may bring. The trunk goes back. Seth?"

"I'll take care of it, Captain."

"Listen, son." Daniel's uncle spoke kindly as he watched Daniel peevishly repack his Gladstone. "You can't go through a winter on the back side in city clothes. We'll get you some good woolens, boots, and slickers."

Daniel was about to say that he was not going to be a surfman and saw no reason to dress like one, but his uncle walked out. Daniel could only pick up his Gladstone and follow. Now he just wanted to end this trip, go to his room to clean up, and have a nap before dinner.

"How far to the station?" he asked.

"About two and a half miles. We usually walk, but since you have baggage, I've asked Wilbur to take us."

A cart with wide-rimmed wheels stood waiting behind the depot. The gray horse between the shafts was dozing and so was the burly driver. The driver had black whiskers and a shirt the color of his horse, but the horse looked well groomed and the man did not.

16

Daniel's uncle said, "Sorry to keep you waiting, Wilbur."

The driver sat up and touched his cap. "Oh, me and Charity, we don't mind a little extra sleep, Captain."

"This is my sister's boy, Daniel Stafford. Daniel, this is Wilbur Ridge. And the good-looking old lady between the shafts is Charity."

"How do, Dan'l?" The driver's smile revealed a gap of three teeth.

Daniel stared at the cart. "Must we ride in that thing?"

"Walk if you'd rather."

Daniel tossed his bag into the cart and crawled up after it. His uncle went on foot. Wilbur gave the mare a tender slap of the reins and she started off, head low, big hoofs clopping. As they went through the village, Daniel recognized the general store, the harness maker, the church and bell tower, the houses with doorsills on the street. Soon they were on an oyster-shell road passing cottages with rose-covered fences. Nothing had changed since Daniel was here as a child. Nothing was a welcome sight.

Daniel asked, "How many people live here now?"

"Same as ever. Two thousand or so."

"Never any change, never any progress," Daniel said. "How do you stand it? Aren't you bored?"

His uncle laughed. "No. Somehow we do pass the time."

"Just plugging along like this old nag, I guess."

The driver spat over the side of his cart. "But we get there just the same, don't we, Captain?"

17

"I wasn't talking to you, driver," Daniel said.

Wilbur turned to squint at Daniel from under his great eyebrows. "No more was I talking to you, sonny."

"The boy's just left home, Wilbur," Daniel's uncle said. "He's a mite out of sorts. Hope you'll pay him no mind."

"It don't bother me nothing, Captain."

Daniel fell silent, annoyed to hear his behavior explained to this man. Daniel was annoyed further when his uncle and the driver began talking together as though he were not there.

"Hear tell the superintendent and the board of examiners come out for inspection," the driver said. "Everything go all right, Captain?"

"Yes, we're in fine shape. Not up to speed with the beach-apparatus drill, but we'll soon have it right."

"Certain you will. No better crew anywhere than Perkins Hollow. But I hear a man at Race Point got let off for age, without a penny's compensation." Wilbur shook his head. "Lifesavers should have pensions, says I, and the same for their widows and orphans. And uniforms, same as the navy. And keepers should have a crew year round. It ain't right to be out there alone in summer, depending on volunteers."

Daniel's uncle laughed. "Wish you could speak for us in Washington. But we'll get it all, one day. For now we're just thankful to have the best equipment there is."

The road became a sandy track through low pines that scraped against the cart. Off in the woods a pond glimmered.

18

"Say, Captain, how's that young feller, your Number Six? Will Ryder by name, I mean."

"Oh, Will is keen. He'll be a captain, one day."

"I didn't mean that. I mean the other thing."

"Does everybody in Fleetport know about the other thing?"

"No, it's just my wife. She thinks it's a pity the Beckers girl has turned against Will. So what is it, Captain? Do you know? Does Ed Beckers ever mention it?"

"No, he doesn't. I have no idea what's wrong."

Wilbur made such a loud cluck of dismay that Charity mistook it for a command and jigged a few steps.

Trees grew farther apart, shrubs became scarce, and patches of dune grass appeared. The cart wheels dragged through sand. The horse began to labor.

"This is close enough, Wilbur," Daniel's uncle said. "Thanks for the help." He gave Charity's neck a thump. "Thanks to you, too, old girl."

Wilbur touched his cap, turned Charity, and they set off back to the village at the same sleepy pace.

With the Gladstone dragging at his arm, Daniel tramped after his uncle. The thunder of breakers and the squeal of gulls depressed him. Sand grew deeper and slipped away under his shoes. He tripped over clumps of grass and began to sweat in the sun.

The path led downward but his uncle turned off uphill. Daniel paused. "Isn't the station below on the beach?"

"We'll take a look at the view before we go down."

The climb grew steeper. The salty smell of ocean

19

came on a breeze that whipped Daniel's hair. Abruptly the brow of a cliff was under Daniel's feet. His knees turned to sponge. He stumbled back.

Heights made Daniel go faint. Even his cycle had made him so giddy at first that he'd thought he would never be able to ride it. But his friend Arthur had been there to urge him on.

"Your body can do this, only your head holds you back. Heights bother some people; nobody knows why. It has nothing to do with courage." Arthur was planning to study something called psychology and he already knew a great deal. "So you mustn't be ashamed or any such rot."

With Arthur's help Daniel had learned to ride his cycle, but he was not cured. And he was still ashamed.

Now from the edge of the cliff, his uncle said, "Come see this view, Daniel."

Daniel forced himself to creep forward but he could not look down at the surf hissing along the shore. He managed to glance left and right at the stretches of beach under rugged bluffs layered in orange, ivory, and rust. Just below on his right was a house with a red roof topped by a flag snapping in the wind. On the cliff beyond was a hut overlooking the sea.

"Straight out there is Portugal," his uncle said. "And nothing between it and Cape Cod but three thousand miles of ocean. I think there can hardly be a more wonderful sight."

Daniel made an effort to look out past the breakers to reefs where calm water was the color of gold and beyond where the sea was emerald and then sapphire. A great purple bow marked the horizon, separating sea and sky. Far out, a schooner in full sail was rising and dipping.

Daniel had never before seen so much ocean. As a child on the beach he had only been aware of sand and stinging surf. Now he felt compelled to look down. Wave after wave was rushing to shore, cresting, tumbling white-capped toward the base of the cliff a hundred feet below. Daniel's head spun. His legs went fizzy. He staggered back. It was a moment before he could follow what his uncle was saying.

"These shores are beautiful and awe inspiring, but dangerous. The coastline and sandbars are always shifting, making old maps worse than useless and even new ones in constant need of revision."

"Can't we go now?" Daniel said.

"I have something to say to you first." The man's sudden look of stern authority so surprised Daniel that he nodded meekly. He disliked himself for it at once.

"Until now it was proper for you to call me uncle. But from this moment you are one of a crew of surfmen under my command. You will address me as sir or Captain Alder."

Daniel rallied. "I thought you weren't allowed another surfman," he said. "I thought six was your quota."

"The district superintendent has let you come because I told him I need another hand and you won't cost us anything. You are not enlisted, but you are to follow every regulation. You will obey orders instantly, cheerfully, and without question, just as my surfmen do. You will be trained as they are and take part in everything but actual rescues. This was the agreement I made with your mother. Is that clear?"

Daniel laughed and gave him a mocking salute. "Yes sir, Captain. Anything you say, sir."

His uncle's great fist clamped on the lapels of Daniel's jacket. Daniel went soaring. Hanging before the hard rock of his uncle's face and his fierce, enormous eyes, Daniel felt as helpless as a rag in the teeth of a mastiff.

"Hear this! As long as you are at my station you will not sneer. You will not laugh unless you hear a joke. What I have just said was no joke. Do you understand?"

Daniel gasped. "Oh yes, sir!"

Daniel was jolted to the ground so hard that his knees gave way and he sank into a patch of dune grass.

Stumbling after his uncle, Daniel felt his resentment rise again. "All right, then, sir," he muttered. "Captain it is." He would not even think of such a brute as his uncle.

FOUR

LUGGING HIS GLADSTONE, Daniel stumbled down the white sand to the station. To him, the station looked like a barn, with ramps leading to two wide doors. Worse, among the tipsy sheds in back was what seemed to be an outhouse. The closer Daniel got, the more depressed he felt. Even the dazzling ocean visible between the cliffs did not cheer him.

A screen door squealed. Three men came out, men like Daniel's uncle with powerful shoulders and rugged faces.

"What took you so long, Captain?" one called.

"Most likely rode with old Charity," another said. The men laughed.

"This is Daniel Stafford," the captain said. He did not add that Daniel was his nephew, but the men must have known that already. Daniel expected them to act accordingly.

They offered huge coarse hands as the captain named them.

Edwin Beckers was as tall as the captain but older, with gray hair and a thick mustache. No doubt he was the father of that Beckers girl Wilbur had talked about.

Ross Ogilvie was younger but just as weathered, with a dark beard and broad yellow teeth clenched about a pipe. He was shorter than the others but he had long arms and a crushing grip.

Will Ryder, about Daniel's size, was a good-looking young fellow, with red-gold hair and a clean-shaven face.

"Glad to have you with us, Daniel," Will said, smiling as though he meant it. Daniel wondered what was wrong with him that had made the Beckers girl reject him.

As they turned back to the station, Ross removed his pipe and squinted at Daniel. "You any good at checkers?"

Will laughed. "Ross wants someone to best our champion. He thinks Abner needs taking down."

"Abner Howe," Edwin said. "He's on watch now, up at the lookout." He indicated the hut on the edge of the cliff.

The men crowded into the station ahead of Daniel. Not a scratch of manners among them, he thought. A warm smell of cinnamon reminded him of how hungry he was.

"This is our galley," Will said. "Kitchen, that is."

24

"I know what galley means," Daniel said. He looked about with contempt. At the far end was a black range flanked by chairs and a hot-water tank. Under a window facing the cliff was an iron sink with a hand pump. A basin and mirror hung beside a cabinet of shaving mugs and razors. Cupboards lined the walls and a huge work-table filled the middle of the room.

A man with a hefty backside was at the range slicing carrots into a pot.

"Obed, here's Daniel!" Edwin Beckers said.

Obed was wearing an apron that nearly reached the floor. He walked forward ponderously, as though middle aged, but his grin and round bright eyes gave him the look of a boy.

Ross said, "Obed Woolsey. He's cook this week."

Obed wiped his hand along the front of his apron and offered it. His hand was gentle and slightly greasy.

"We been waiting for you and watching for you all day, Danny. I made codfish chowder, just for you."

"That's Obed's specialty," Edwin said. "He does a master job on it."

"I made rhubarb pudding, too. Do you like rhubarb pudding, Danny?"

Daniel looked at the big man with aversion. "My name is not Danny, it's Daniel." He turned to the captain, who stood at the door, hands in pockets, looking on. "I'd like to go to my room now and have a bath and a rest before dinner."

The men glanced at one another and then at the captain. Still smiling, Obed filled the pause. "We already had dinner. Dinner's at midday. Next we have supper."

The captain said, "Number Six, please show Daniel where to leave his things."

"Yes, sir," Will said.

"He can have a wash. Then show him the boat room and explain our equipment." The captain turned to Daniel. "After that, you are to help Obed with supper."

Daniel was about to protest that he was tired, but the captain's eyes had such a dangerous glint that he decided to wait until he and the captain were alone to speak his mind. He followed Will out to a large room next to the galley.

"This is our mess," Will said. "That door leads to the captain's office. The boat room is through that big door opposite. We men sleep upstairs."

The mess looked as tidy as a ship. The bare floor was scrubbed chalk white. A polished brass lamp hung above a table and clumsy chairs. Near the boat-room door was a barometer next to a clock. A print of a clip-per ship was on the wall above a writing table and book-shelves. Behind faded curtains, the windows sparkled.

"As you see, we're quite comfortable here," Will said.

"Comfortable? I don't even see a stove or fireplace."

"Oh, the range in our galley gives all the heat we need."

Will led him up spiral stairs to a room under bare rafters. The room had three dormer windows on one side and two doors on the other, five cots in a row with sea chests at the foot, hooks on the wall for jackets and pants. Near the stairs was a cot with sheets and blankets folded at the head and a rickety-looking table.

"That's your place, Daniel," Will said. "The captain has a sea chest for you, and Obed found the table for your schoolwork."

Daniel snorted. Was he expected to sleep and study in such surroundings?

"What's through those two doors?" he demanded.

"On the right is Number One's room. He's second in command. On the left is our infirmary."

Daniel threw open the door on the left and found a narrow room with cupboards and six made-up cots.

He dropped his bag. "I guess this will do."

"Sorry, this is reserved for the sick or injured. We keep it ready with beds, spare clothing, and medical supplies."

"Why should we all be crowded together when this place is empty? It doesn't make sense."

"It does to us. We're a rescue station."

"We'll see about that. But first I want a bath."

"We bathe on Saturday. But you can wash in the galley."

Will's mild replies raised Daniel's scorn. No doubt the fellow was intimidated by him as the captain's nephew.

Will turned away. "I'll wait for you in the mess."

Daniel flopped down on the cot and clutched his head. When he became aware again that he was tired, hungry, and grimy, he dug out a fresh shirt and went downstairs.

Ross was idling in the doorway of the galley, smoking his pipe. Obed was kneading dough, up to his fat elbows in flour.

"I need to wash this soot off," Daniel muttered.

Obed said, "Sure, Danny. Go right on over to the sink."

The men made no move to give him privacy. The washbasin looked clean, although chipped, but the soap was harsh and the only towel was coarse and suspiciously damp. Daniel found washing a disgusting experience. He put on his clean shirt and held out the soiled one. "What do I do with this?"

Ross blew a cloud of smoke. "Wash it or toss it."

"We do our wash on Saturday, Danny," Obed said.

Daniel clamped the shirt under his arm and went to the mess. To Will he said, "Where's my—where's the captain?"

"In his office. We're supposed to knock."

Daniel went to the captain's door and yanked it open. He was startled by a roar. "Out!"

Face suddenly flaming, Daniel closed the door.

"Try knocking," Will suggested, and did it for him.

"Come in," the captain said quietly.

The captain's room combined office with desk and files; bedroom with four poster and patchwork counterpane; parlor with rug, rocking chairs, and shelves of books, among which stood a photograph of the woman Daniel remembered as Aunt Mercy. It must have been she who had furnished this room during her summers

28

here with the captain before she died. Now the captain had the coziest room in the station all to himself.

The captain was going through papers. "Settled in?"

Daniel said, "I insist on my rights as a gentleman. I will not do laundry. I will not work in the galley. I'm tired and I want the spare room upstairs."

The captain did not trouble to look up. "If you're tired, go to bed. But if you don't work, you don't eat."

"What!"

"I thought it was clear how things will be here. You will sleep where assigned. You will wash your own clothes and bedding. You will do your share of housekeeping, cooking, and polishing equipment. You will take part in drills, patrols, and watches. You will learn your duties as fast as possible, because until then you are a hindrance to the crew."

"But—"

The captain gave Daniel that glare of his that allowed no argument. "Didn't I tell you how to respond to my orders?"

Daniel mumbled, "Well, but . . ."

"I said instantly, cheerfully, and without question. Let's hear it."

Daniel fumed but finally said, "Yes, sir."

"Report to Number Six."

Daniel thought of marching stubbornly to bed, but his hunger prevailed. He followed Will to the huge boat room where the ceiling was two stories high. It housed two flat-bottomed boats on carriages, a cart, and a great deal of gear—ropes, anchors, grapnels, and various tools—all neatly stored. Lockers and benches lined the far wall.

"The lockers are for our slickers and boots," Will said. "Yours is the one at the end."

"I don't wear slickers and boots," Daniel said.

Will did not seem to hear that. He thumped one of the boats fondly. "These are called surfboats, designed for rescues. They're twenty-five feet long with a seven-foot beam, white cedar, very light for their size, only about a thousand pounds, easy to move and handle. This one is for six oars. The other is for five oars and is mainly used in drills."

Accustomed as Daniel was to a racing shell, these rowboats looked enormous. On four-wheeled carriages, they towered over his head.

"Besides crew, these boats can carry twelve people lying on the bottom, or even fifteen in an emergency," Will said. "We keep everything aboard, oars, boat hooks, life belts, ready for action."

Daniel could not help feeling in awe of the boats, which were unlike any he had ever seen. "No rudder?"

"They're steered by an oar, eighteen feet long. It takes a powerful man to handle that in a storm."

"Who steers?"

"The captain. Or Number One." Will slapped the gunwale. "These boats can weather almost anything. They're a beautiful sight in the breakers. Wait till you see!"

Unlike some of the other surfmen, Will was well spoken. It did not make Daniel care for the man.

The cart also looked ready for action, with a huge reel of hawser and other gear neatly stowed, no space wasted even on the sides, where axes, buckets, shovels, lanterns, and a speaking trumpet were hung.

"This is our breeches-buoy apparatus. Those wide tires on the wheels are to help keep the cart from sinking into the sand. It's a beast to pull in a storm, just the same."

"You have to pull this yourselves?"

Will grinned. "Your chance will come." He pointed out a small cannon of polished bronze. "Our new Lyle gun. Isn't she a beauty? She can reach the sandbars almost anywhere along this coast—shoots much farther than our old cast-iron gun. Weighs less, too, only 185 pounds. Two men can carry her easily."

Daniel sneered. "What's it for? Pirates?"

Will's smile was tolerant. "For shooting a line to a wreck when we can't get a boat out. Here's the shot line."

He showed Daniel a rope wound on pegs in a box. "We tie this line to the eye of the shot and it plays out when the cannon is fired. Men aboard the wreck tie the line to the mainmast, and we haul out the breeches buoy and bring survivors back one at a time."

Daniel was impressed in spite of himself.

Will went on, "You'll see how it works next drill. We have beach-apparatus drill Monday and Thursday, boat drill Tuesday, signal-flag drill Wednesday, and on Friday we have emergency care and resuscitation; that's a procedure to restore the breathing of drowning victims."

It seemed like a lot of drilling, Daniel thought, but some of it might be worth learning. At any rate, as long as he was here talking to Will, he didn't have to go work with that oaf in the galley. He began asking questions but failed to pay attention to the answers. Finally, Will gave him a shrewd look and turned away. "Report to Obed."

FIVE

OBED BROKE INTO HIS DIMPLED GRIN. "Glad to have your help, Danny!"

"I'm not used to this, you know," Daniel said. "I don't do this kind of work at home."

Obed wiped his big hands down the front of his apron. He looked puzzled.

"Anyway, I'm stuck here, so what shall I do?"

Obed's smile reappeared. "Take that apron behind the door, Danny. Don't spoil your good clothes."

"I do not wear aprons. Just tell me what to do."

"Let's see. You could slice bread. Cut thick slices, that's how we like it."

The bread was warm and smelled delicious. Daniel was tempted to gobble some down at once, but he was determined not to be pleased by anything. "Now what?"

"Set the table. That's a good idea. Spoons and knives in that drawer. Dishes in the cupboard."

33

Daniel loaded a tray and carried it to the mess. Will, Ross, and Edwin were there and so was another man, sitting near the window with a book. Daniel braced himself for a teasing about his degrading chore, but no one paid any attention.

Ross was reading aloud from a newspaper. "The vessel breaks up. One sailor paddles to shore on a plank and hollers at men on the beach, 'What town is this?' 'Chatham!' they yell. The sailor cries, 'I'll not set foot in Chatham. I'd sooner go down with my brig.' And he heads for the open sea."

Ross slapped his thigh and brayed with laughter.

"Sailor must have come from Harwick," Edwin said with a grin. "Harwick never set store by Chatham."

"I calculate he come from Boston." Ross leered at Daniel. "Seems like folks there don't set store by nothing."

"Stow it, Ross," Edwin said. He turned to the man at the window. "Jon, here's Daniel Stafford. Daniel, meet Jonathan Pilgrim."

"How do you do, Daniel?" Jon half rose and offered his hand. Daniel stared at him in disbelief. Jon was no darker than the other sun-browned surfmen, but he looked different, with huge dark eyes, strong facial bones, and glossy black hair in a short pigtail.

"Pilgrim?" Daniel sneered. He would show these men that he, too, could poke fun. "You don't look like a Pilgrim to me. Any more than our housekeeper's red cat."

Daniel glanced about for the expected laugh, but the

34

men looked blank. Slow-witted, Daniel thought. He would have to make his meaning clear. "But you don't look like a redskin, either, no feathers. You don't even talk like a redskin."

Only Jon looked amused. "How do redskins talk?"

"Me gottum bow! Shootum bear!" Daniel gave a war whoop.

He was cut off by a growl. A great Newfoundland dog jumped up from behind Jon's chair. Her eyes were two sparks of anger, focused on Daniel.

Daniel stumbled back. The men laughed.

"It's all right, girl," Jon said, pressing the dog's shaggy neck. "This is Daniel. He's going to be one of us."

"Your beast has no sense of humor," Daniel said.

Ross grinned. "Certain she has. She knows what's funning and what ain't."

Will intervened. "Jon, may I tell Daniel how you got your name?" With a nod from Jon, Will went on. "One of Jon's ancestors was out hunting alone and broke his leg. A paleface who rescued him called himself a Pilgrim, and Jon's ancestor thought that was the man's name. To show his gratitude he took the name for himself and his family ever after."

Daniel scoffed. "That can't be. Daniel Webster named the Pilgrims. Before that they were called Forefathers."

"By their descendants," Edwin said. "But William Bradford called his people Pilgrims from the start."

Ross blew a cloud of smoke. "It sure do surprise me that folks from Boston don't know all there is."

Obed appeared. "Jon! Abner wants you in the look-out."

Jon leaped up. Daniel was astonished at how tall he was, taller than any of the others, and at how quickly he moved. His dog scrabbled after him, huge paws slipping on the floor.

The men jumped up, too, ready for action it seemed, but Obed came back carrying a tureen of chowder and said that Jon had signaled there was no problem.

The men went to the table and stood behind their chairs. The captain came out of his office to the head of the table.

"We'll wait for Number One," he said.

"Isn't Edwin Number One?" Daniel asked Obed.

"No, Jon is Number One. He's in charge when the captain ain't here. Ed is Number Two. He's in charge when the captain and Number One ain't here both. Ross is Number Three. He's in charge when . . ." Obed gave up the rest of his thought. "Abner is Number Four. I'm Number Five. Will is Number Six."

The men were looking at Obed in fond amusement.

"And what is Danny?" Obed asked the men. "Number Seven?"

"He can't be Number Seven," Ross said. "Trueheart is Number Seven. She's as good a lifesaver as any of us."

"Then is Danny Number Eight?"

"Not yet, he ain't. He's more like Seven and a Half."

"Much as I admire True," Edwin said, smiling, "I think it's wrong to rank man or boy below a dog."

Ross laughed. "Then Daniel can be Six and a Half."

36

Daniel looked to the captain for support, but he seemed lost in thought. Jon came back and stood at the foot of the table. His dog trotted to her mat and settled down, head on her forepaws.

"Jon, have you met Daniel?" the captain asked.

Jon nodded. "We're glad to have you with us, Daniel. We hope you will be happy here."

Daniel did not respond. He felt shamed by Jon's courtesy in the face of his rudeness. He did not like being outdone as a gentleman, but having taken an attitude, he found it hard to relent.

The men stood with heads bowed while the captain said a prayer of thanks for the food, for help in their duties, and for the welfare of families. Daniel was hungry and irked by the delay, but there was no sign of impatience from the men, not a sigh, not a shuffle of feet. Even though he had always gone to church with his mother and Mrs. O'Till, prayer of such quiet intensity was unfamiliar to him. In his view, women were the religious ones and men their yawning escorts.

Daniel found Obed's chowder and bread even better than Mrs. O'Till's, but the company nearly took away his appetite. Most of the men bent low over their bowls, made smacking and gulping noises, snatched things across the table, talked with mouths full of bread, teased, guffawed, and slapped one another on the back.

Compared to these men, the captain seemed fit for society, and so, to Daniel's surprise, did Jon. Jon sat up straight, chewed modestly, asked for things politely. Jon did not laugh aloud and even his smile was reserved. Jon slapped no one and no one slapped him.

When the captain asked for attention, silence fell at once. "I have last year's figures for our district."

Obed broke in. "Cape Cod is District Two, Danny. We got nine stations in District Two."

The captain spoke from a note. "Disasters, twenty. Vessels and cargo entirely lost, ten. Value of property lost, $69,530. Property saved, $24,604. Persons lost, nineteen."

"Nineteen!" Obed cried. "Oh, that's a pity!"

"But persons saved, a hundred and two," the captain said.

To Daniel, Will said, "Before the Life-Saving Service, almost everybody wrecked on these shores was lost."

"Best to think on how we have improved things," Edwin said.

"Excuse me, please," the captain said. "I have reports to finish." He went to his office.

"Didn't even wait for his pudding," Obed said.

"He'd be done with reports by now if he'd let me do the errands in town today," Ross said. "It was my turn."

Daniel thought, So the men resent the captain's iron hand as much as I do.

Will said, "Never mind, Ross. You can have my turn on Thursday."

Ross grinned. "Ain't you got somebody special to see there no more?"

"Belay that, Ross," Edwin said.

"Sorry, Ross, but Will goes on Thursday," Jon said. "The captain has a particular errand for him."

Ed interposed, "Say, Number One, what's this I hear about a challenge from Pamet River?"

Jon nodded. "They mean to do the beach drill in less than four minutes before Thanksgiving. If we beat their record, they'll send us a couple of turkeys."

"We will beat them, or we'll give them their whole Thanksgiving dinner," Edwin said.

"And I'll cook!" Obed cried.

"Don't say that, Obed, or we might throw the contest."

The men's laughter became a roar. Cheers exploded in thundering baritone and brazen tenor. Daniel was astonished at the sound. He saw the men suddenly as a troop of giants with huge shoulders and great powerful arms rippling with muscle. He struggled against feeling like a child among them.

"Hold on, surfmen," Jon said. "Don't celebrate yet. The best we've done so far is six minutes."

"We can beat that," Will said. "We'll set a new record for the whole service."

"What's the old record?" Obed asked.

Jon said, "According to the General Superintendent—"

Obed put in, "That's Sumner Kimball in Washington, D.C., Danny. He's in charge of the service on all coasts."

"Shut up for once, Obed," Ross said. "Let Jon talk."

"Kimball said he wouldn't believe it if he hadn't seen it. From the command for action till the victim was down off the wreck pole . . ." Jon paused, glancing at the expectant faces.

"Go on, Jon! Don't keep us hanging," Ed said.

"Two minutes, thirty seconds."

Obed gasped. "Who done it? What station?"

"Kimball didn't say."

"Not Pamet River, I'll bet my suspenders." Ross laughed.

"But Pamet River's got the edge on us," Will said. "They've already passed inspection."

"You mean they've done it in five minutes?" Ross asked.

"That they have," Will said. "But my mother wrote me that they drill with the whole crew. They don't use one of their surfmen to play victim. The captain's wife goes over from Truro and climbs the wreck pole herself."

"It's wrong to make her do that," Obed said.

"She volunteered. The district superintendent said it was all right. We save women and children, same as men."

"Even before men," Ed said.

"My wife would play victim," Ross said. "But knowing her size, I'd be afraid she'd wreck the apparatus."

"Shame on you, Ross," Ed said. The men laughed.

Ross said, "I got a better idea. Let Six and a Half do it."

Daniel's heart began to pound with alarm.

"It's fun, Danny," Obed said. "You get to climb up the wreck pole and ride down in the breeches buoy."

"It's a nice long ride to the ground." Ross grinned. "The pole is forty feet high."

Edwin spoke kindly. "Forty feet is easy, son. Sailors climb a hundred, two hundred feet and think nothing."

"And we have a crow's-nest on top," Will said. "Some stations only have a yardarm."

Ross stroked his beard and looked at Daniel with glee, as though he knew that Daniel's palms were sweating and his stomach was in a knot. Ross was baiting him and the others were reassuring, but Daniel suspected that they all saw him not as a superior gentleman, but as a weak, pampered dandy from the city.

Daniel tried to reassure himself. The men would soon learn that although they were bigger and older, he was a superb athlete who could row as well as any of them and do anything else they could do except climb poles. Meanwhile he would find some way to hide his problem with heights. That was something these brutes would never understand.

SIX

THE MEN WERE STILL SITTING around the table, exulting over how they would beat Pamet River, when Jon said, "Will, please tell Abner he can come down to supper. We'll start patrol." Ed, Jon, and his dog went off to the boat room.

"This week they patrol sunset till eight," Obed said. He seemed to have appointed himself Daniel's tutor. "Ed goes north toward Pamet River. Jon and Trueheart go south toward Nauset. Next Ross and Will patrol eight o'clock till midnight. Then Abner and the captain—"

"The captain patrols like the rest of you?"

"Certain he does. Then Jon and Ed go again, four A.M. till sunrise."

"Twice in one night?"

"We all do that, in turn. We patrol days besides, if it's too foggy to see from the watch house. But I don't patrol this week because I'm cook."

Ross said, "Obed, give your jaw a rest and get some chowder for Abner."

Boots clumped through the galley. A man with wheat-colored hair and a long mustache came in. He looked Ross's age, but tall and lean, all sinews and heavy bones.

"This must be Daniel," he said in a hearty bass. "I'm Abner Howe. Ross, you scoundrel, I hope you left me some bread. Obed! Where's that chowder?"

Obed brought in a full tureen and a new loaf of bread. Abner tore great bites from the loaf alternating with slurps of chowder. Daniel saw Ross had that glint in his eye that preceded a hard time for somebody.

"Better look out, Abner. Daniel here means to best you at checkers."

"I don't play children's games," Daniel said.

Ross laughed. "More airs than a country stud horse."

Daniel was glad when the captain summoned him.

"I've put you on the duty roster," the captain said. "This week you will help Obed and take part in the drills. Next week you will go with Obed on patrol."

"When am I supposed to study?" Daniel demanded. Even studying seemed better than the captain's roster.

"After you've learned our routines. On Thursday Will goes to Fleetport to get you some winter clothes."

"I want to go myself. If I have to wear such clothes, I insist they fit. Sir!"

"You're not dressing for society. Will can get what you need. Tell him your boot size. For the rest, what fits him will fit you."

Fuming, Daniel turned away, but then he remembered his more pressing worry. "About the beach drill, sir. The men want me to be victim, but—"

"Good idea. How are you with knots?"

"Knots, sir? Grandfather taught me all about knots."

"Good. Will can help you review them. And he'll explain your duties in the drill."

"But Captain, sir, please, I can't—"

"We do not use that word here. Get back to your duties."

Daniel had a desperate impulse to fall at the captain's feet and confess his panic. But his pride intervened.

Daniel found Obed at the sink, up to his elbows in suds. Drying spoons but absorbed by anxiety, Daniel hardly knew that he muttered his thoughts.

"It's all his fault. He's a mean one, that Ross. He's mean about everybody and everything."

Obed looked surprised. "Why, no he ain't, Danny. He just teases till he gets it back and then he laughs the more."

"His wife wasn't here to give it back when he said she'd break the beach apparatus."

"He was joking. Ross is proud of her and their two boys, all big and strong the same. She knows how he feels."

Daniel scoffed. Obed was too simple to see the truth.

"Ross don't say nothing behind a person that he won't say to his face," Obed went on. "He don't mean bad in it. But some things he don't never josh about.

44

Not Abner's boy that's sickly, nor Ed's sister that's not in good sense, nor the captain's wife he misses sore, nor Jon so poor because he gives his pay to his widow sister in Mashpee."

Daniel felt a headache coming on. "All right. Ross is a prince. I concede."

Obed smiled at him. "You talk good, Danny. I expect you got book learning plenty. You'll be right to home here with our crew, all smart like you. All but me, that is. Lucky it don't take booklore to be an ordinary surf-man. But I did get to third grade. Abner and Ross, they both got to sixth grade. Ed went to fisherman's school as a lad and then maritime school. Will and the captain went clear through high school. But Jon did the most. Jon went to Harvard."

"You don't mean Harvard. Indians don't go to Harvard."

"Certain they do. Jon says the first Indian graduated more than two hundred year ago."

"I don't believe it. I don't believe half Jon says."

Obed held a plate suspended, dripping suds. His eyes went big. "Jon don't lie, Danny. That's terrible to say."

"All right. Ross is a prince. Jon is a pundit. Every surfman here has a head full of learning. If you say so."

Obed smiled, happy again. "The captain and Jon need all their learning, with paperwork and plenty, logs to keep every day, and reports on every wreck and res-cue. Even the weather, sea, and surf. And all about our drills, patrols and watches, supplies we use, how much soap and coal. The General Superintendent is a mighty one for details. I'm glad I'll never have to be captain, or Number One, either. I like just what I am, Number Five. I was Number Six till Will came and I got promoted. My grandma was so proud."

"How much more pay did you get?"

"No more pay. We all get the same. Except the captain."

"That doesn't sound like much of a promotion."

"But it ain't the money, don't you see?"

When they had polished the stove and scrubbed the tables and the galley floor, Daniel thought their work was done at last, but Obed said, "Now we fix something for the men coming off patrol. But I'll do that, Danny. You sit and rest a spell."

Relaxing in a chair by the stove, eyes closed and head back, Daniel hardly minded that Obed went on talking about what the men did off-season. Vaguely Daniel heard that Obed helped his grandmother with her chickens and garden and did some work for the blacksmith. Will was a reporter for a newspaper in Provincetown. Jon was a hunting and fishing guide for summer sportsmen. Then Obed was shaking him.

"Go to bed, Danny. You must be tired, your first day."

But in the dormitory, Daniel could not sleep. He was bothered by the roar of the breakers, the swish and pause of surf. His cot was narrow, his mattress lumpy. Dread of the beach drill caused him a fearful round of thoughts about running away, pretending to be sick, trying again to plead his case.

He must have slept at last, however, because it seemed much later when he was aroused by whispering. A shadow cast by candlelight danced over the walls. The shadow became Abner pulling off his boots, whispering to Ed. Jon came from his room followed by his dog. Trueheart's claws and Jon's boots clattered on the stairs. The candle was snuffed out. Moonlight shimmered at the windows. Abner's snores filled the room, keeping Daniel awake with his fears.

SEVEN

"TIME TO GET UP, DANNY." It was not yet dawn, but there was Obed standing over him. Remembering that he was one day closer to disaster, Daniel tried to bury himself, but Obed stripped off his blanket.

"I'll go stoke the fire," Obed said.

By the time Daniel got down to the galley, the range was blazing and the smell of brewing coffee was almost enough to cheer him. Obed was stirring batter at the worktable. He looked up with his eager smile.

"Good morning, Danny."

"It doesn't look good to me." Through the galley window Daniel could see mist crawling over the beach. Surf was subdued, breakers muffled. Behind banks of rolling clouds, scraps of a rosy horizon tinged the sea. A foghorn blared.

"Bread's in the oven and the corned beef is boiling,"

Obed said. "Think I'll make a brown Betty for dinner. Would you like that, Danny?"

Daniel could not raise his spirits enough to answer.

Only Will and Ross appeared for breakfast. Ross said the blessing quietly with no sign of joking, eyes tightly closed. The men piled up griddlecakes and smeared on gobs of butter.

Obed said, "Looks like you got to patrol this morning, don't it, Ross?"

"Patrol till it clears, leastways," Ross said.

"Will it clear?"

Daniel spoke to Will, avoiding Ross, but Ross answered with a laugh. "Always has."

Obed giggled. "That's a good'un!"

"That's an old one," Will said. "Don't mind Ross, Daniel. He thinks any old joke is better than none."

Grasping hope, Daniel said, "If it doesn't clear up by tomorrow, I guess we call off the beach drill, don't we?"

Ross popped his eyes in mock astonishment. "Does Six and a Half think we only save people when the sun shines?"

"We go out in fog more often than any other weather," Will said. "Fog is the cause of most wrecks, because it hides the rips and shoals that run all along this coast."

"Rips are rough water where currents cross," Obed said.

Anxiety and pique made Daniel feel a need to assert himself. "I know that. My grandfather taught me all there is to know about this coast."

Ross laughed. "We got the wrong man as Number One."

The outer door blew open. Ed, in slickers and high rubber boots, came in stamping and rubbing his hands.

"Turn cold, did it?" Will asked.

"Not as cold as it's going to."

Obed laughed. "That's a good'un."

"That's an old one," Ross said.

Ed went on to the boat room. The outer door flew open again and Jon's dog rushed past to the galley. With a nod for the men, Jon followed her.

Obed said, "Jon feeds Trueheart first, then himself. She's his patrol mate, and she's a good'un."

"She's pulled more than one man out of the surf," Ross said. "Alive or dead, it don't matter to her."

"Oh, it matters," Will said. "But she knows we want them either way. That dog will swim out to save anything. Saved a ship's cat last year. Even saved a parrot once."

"That parrot swore in cockney, funniest thing you ever heard. I wanted to keep it to liven up the place." Ross chuckled. "Too bad we had to save its master."

Obed frowned. "It's wrong to say that, even funning."

Ross grinned. "What's wrong with funning?"

As they cleaned up after breakfast, Obed said, "Today is signal-flag drill, Danny. We use flags for messages. Some day we'll have wires for the telegraph and telephone like the stations in North Carolina. They can talk by wire to anywhere, even Washington, D.C. Ain't that a miracle?"

The men assembled in the mess for the drill, which turned out to be exercises with bits of colored tin.

"These are for practice," Obed said. "For real we have big flags in the same shapes and colors, standing for letters, numbers, or a whole message."

The men came to attention with Jon and Trueheart facing them. Jon said, "Number Five, please tell Daniel the basics."

Obed nodded eagerly. "A message is called a hoist, because the flags are hoisted on a halyard. The message is not English or any other language. It's in code, and every language has its own codebook."

Daniel still felt a need to prove himself. "Never mind basics. I know the basics from sailing with my grandfather."

"Seems like Six and a Half don't have nothing to learn," Ross said. "Seems like he ought to be captain."

"If you don't believe me, I'll tell you," Daniel said. "Yellow means sickness aboard. Red means mutiny. Black means pirates."

"Did once," Edwin said. "But now it means a lawful execution has been carried out on board."

"What good is it to know that?" Daniel said. "I bet none of you has ever even seen it."

"I have," Edwin said. "It is not a happy sight."

Jon said, "But which signals are our main concern?"

"Signals of distress," Obed said. "Besides flags, a vessel might fire a gun every minute, sound a foghorn without stopping, shoot red flares, or burn a fire on board."

Jon flashed the tin flags and called on the men in turn to say which numbers or letters they stood for. The men snapped out their answers. Even Obed's replies were immediate. Daniel could not raise his hand fast enough when something he knew came up. When slates and chalk were handed out and the men given signals to write, Daniel was at a loss.

"Don't tell me we found something Six and a Half don't know," Ross said, grinning. Daniel could not wait for some chance to prove himself at something.

After dinner, Will reminded Daniel that they were to review knots. Daniel asked to do it outdoors, claiming to need air after being cooped up in the galley, but in truth he did not want to perform in front of the crew. Will collected ropes and a shovel and they set out.

By now the sky was sharply blue and the sun warm. Daniel became aware again of the breakers and their booming echo along the cliffs. Gulls paraded and pecked on the beach. A wedge of Canada geese passed overhead, already fleeing from winter, but for the moment it was summer still.

Daniel had a flash of joy, a memory of running to the sea with his bucket, hot sand between his toes, the exhilarating sting of spray. But the joy was gone in a moment. That was the past and this was the present, with fearful prospects.

Will stopped at the base of a dune and stuck his shovel up in the sand. "We'll practice hitching the rope to this. Call it the wreck pole."

"This is a waste of time," Daniel said. "I've been tying knots since I was three years old."

"With life and death at stake?"

"What's that supposed to mean?"

"You'll know when you're out in a storm, blinded by sleet and blowing sand, and your mittens are stiff with ice. You hear a vessel cracking up on the bars and sailors screaming in the rigging and their only hope is in your speed and skill with the breeches buoy."

Daniel was sobered by Will's grave expression. "That's happened to you?"

"Twice last year, my first year as a surfman. Sometimes I was so frightened and exhausted that my mind went blank, but I could do the job anyway, thanks to our training. I asked Ed when a surfman stops being afraid. He said never. I almost decided then that my first year would be my last."

"But you stayed. Why?"

"We lost a man the first time and it was awful, but the next time we saved everybody with the breeches buoy. When we got the last man ashore we all burst into tears, even Jon. There are not many jobs where your work counts for more."

"I see that. I don't deny it. But I won't be in on rescues. Knots won't mean life and death to me."

"Don't be so sure. You have to hitch the gear to the wreck pole yourself before you come down in the breeches buoy. I think you'll want to get it right."

EIGHT

THE NEXT MORNING THE CAPTAIN announced that the beach drill would be delayed. Daniel was flooded with hope, but hope drained away with the captain's next words.

"We'll wait for Will to get back from town."

Daniel followed the captain to his office. He intended to make a last plea to be excused from the drill, but when he met the captain's iron gaze, he knew there would be no reprieve. He had only one desperate idea left.

"Will's going to buy my clothes, isn't he? I want to go with him, sir."

"We have already discussed that. Permission denied. When you finish in the galley, you will stand watch with Ed until we're ready for drill."

Daniel found Will in the dormitory, putting on a necktie for town. Daniel said, "I'm going with you." He took his jacket, hat, and purse.

"Do you have permission?" Will asked.

Daniel glared at him.

"I didn't think so," Will said. "The only time more than one man goes to town is for church."

"That doesn't make sense."

"It does to us. We could be called out any minute."

"You got along without me before, so I don't see—"

"In the service, we must all share alike."

"What if I go? Will I be flogged? Court-martialed?"

Will's gaze was mild with sympathy. "What's the matter, Daniel? It can't be just the clothes."

Daniel felt shamed by Will's caring response to his rudeness, and by something else, the sense that it would be cowardly to run away.

Will did not press him for an answer, but saw his change of heart. "I'll do my best for you, Daniel," he said.

After cleanup, Daniel went out to stand watch with Edwin as ordered. The sun felt good on his back as he crossed the beach, but it did not help the chill of fear in his bones, the sense of approaching disaster.

Close up, the cliff looked even steeper and more perilous than it did from a distance. Logs were set as steps, but they were too far apart and the rope strung on posts as a handrail seemed to offer little security. Still, the cliff would not be as dangerous as the wreck pole he was expected to climb later. Maybe he could manage it.

After four steps, however, his legs began to tingle. Daniel set his jaw and hauled himself up by the man-rope step after step. The wind grew bolder, ruffled his

hair. His shoes slipped on a sandy log and he saved himself only by his sweaty hold on the rope. Head spinning,
he had to stop and hang on until he could raise the
strength to climb again. At last he could see the dune
grass on top of the cliff.

He fell forward, scrambled away from the edge, and
sat in the grass breathing hard. His despair returned. He
had mastered the cliff for now, but not his dread.

After a moment he got to the watch house, a sturdy
hut of silver-gray shingles, windows to seaward, and a
door to the lee. Ed was writing at a tall desk, with a spyglass on a tripod beside him and binoculars hanging on
the wall. He looked up with a smile. His gray hair and
mustache contrasted sharply with his face, which was
tanned the color of cedar.

"Glad to have you, Dan." Ed was milder than his
rowdy friends, Abner and Ross. "Be with you as soon as
I post this."

Daniel glanced about. Charts of flags and silhouettes
of ships with smokestacks were on the back wall.
Windows on the other three sides were open to the
breeze. The glass was milky with pits and scratches.

"What's the matter with your windowpanes?" Daniel
asked.

"Etched by sand and wind. We have to put new glass
in regularly. The same with our lanterns." Ed put down
his pen. "Come see the view."

Daniel was not eager to see the view, but in the hut
he felt safe enough to step forward. He had a shock of
pleasure at the sight of the great stretch of ocean,

sparkling whitecaps tumbling in endlessly toward the beach.

Although Daniel appreciated the view, he felt a persistent need to assert himself among these men. "I don't see much point in keeping watch on a day like this."

"Trouble doesn't always wait for bad weather. But trouble or no, we have to record every passing vessel. There's a lot to watch, with so much traffic on these shores."

"Captain's orders so you won't fall asleep up here." Daniel hoped Ed would admit the captain was unreasonable.

"Oh, it's not the captain's orders. The orders come from Washington. Every station follows them, so that if a vessel fails to appear on schedule, we'll know where to look."

"Well, it's boring I'm sure, but not hard. I could do it. My grandfather taught me to recognize everything, schooner, bark, barkentine, clipper, brig, brigantine; I know them all."

"Good. What do you see out there now?"

"Three fishing smacks, a schooner, and a sloop."

"What about that vessel farther out, heading north?"

"Oh, yes. Two masts, square rigging, a brig, of course."

"Actually, she's a snow. Take the glass and you'll see the fore-and-aft trysail at the bowsprit."

"Right," Daniel said. Although his grandfather had mentioned snows, this one was the first Daniel had ever seen.

"We don't see many snows, nowadays," Ed said.

"That's just what I was going to say."

"On his last raid, the pirate Black Sam Bellamy captured a snow. The pirates got so drunk on stolen Madeira that the captain of the snow managed to lure Bellamy's vessel onto the shoals and down she went. The *Whydah*, that was. She's out there now, two miles offshore. We see a bit of her now and then, when the sandbar shifts. They'll have her up, one day."

They stood together, looking out.

"Here comes a sweetheart of a clipper," Ed said. He gave Daniel the binoculars. "Have a look."

The clipper was rising and dipping under great wings of sail. Spray broke and glittered over her figurehead, a girl with white skirts, painted cheeks, and flowing golden hair.

Daniel remembered that he and his grandfather had loved clippers. Vividly he saw the rough kindly face of his grandfather, the white eyebrows, sea blue eyes, broad skillful hands that Daniel had loved to watch at work. Daniel felt an ache for the loss of him as he had not felt for years.

"Would you note the clipper in the log, Dan?"

Daniel enjoyed making a careful record as Ed dictated.

"We see less sail and more steam every year," Ed said. "Some day the clippers will be lost from the seas forever."

Ed fell silent, only now and then asking Daniel's help. Was that a barkentine? A naval vessel? Would he identify that steamship by its smokestack from the chart on the wall?

Wind buffeted the watch house but the sun kept it warm. Soothed by the man's serenity, Daniel began to acknowledge his kindness and intelligence. He could respect such a man, who did his job faithfully and gave the other fellow his due. He rather liked being called Dan, at any rate better than Danny.

He was taken aback when Ed asked, "Why don't you like it here with us, Dan?"

Daniel did not answer. Ed went on, "Most young people love the station. My daughter Fannie thinks it's great fun. She'd join the service if girls were allowed. I think she'd make a good'un." He laughed and turned the spyglass to sea. "My older daughter, Rachel, doesn't want to come out these days." He sighed. "Of course, she's a young lady now and has other interests." Ed wrote in his log. "Maybe you have other interests, too."

"I have, but my mother made me give them up."

"I suppose she thought she had a reason."

Daniel knew that, but it did not make his troubles easier to bear. "Nobody cares how I feel."

After another silence, Ed surprised him again. "I think it's not so much that you don't like it here. It's more that you don't want to like it here."

Daniel said, "I don't see what difference that makes."

"I think you will if you think about it."

"You mean I won't let myself like it here because that would be admitting my mother was right."

"That's hard on you, not your mother. And you might miss something good."

Recognizing that as true did not ease Daniel's feelings, especially now that they were complicated by fear. He had an impulse to pour out his problem to Ed.

But Ed said, "Will's calling you. Better go."

Now Daniel had to climb down the cliff, which was worse than going up. He went to the edge cautiously. Grasping the top post, he turned to go backward so that he could keep his eyes on the logs and resist the urge to look down at the beach and the crawling surf. Feeling for each step with the toe of his shoe, he went slowly, clutching the manrope with both hands. Wind lifted sand from the dune and blew it in his face. He shivered. His legs threatened to buckle. At last, trembling in every muscle, he found the beach under his shoes. He bent over the steps, gasping, unable to let go of the rope.

"Daniel, are you all right?" Will offered his support.

Daniel straightened. "I don't need your help."

Will looked at him uncertainly, then said, "Your new clothes are on your bed. You can change before drill."

Daniel found wool shirts and trousers, long underwear, a thick jacket, cap, scarf, suspenders, mittens, oilskins, high rubber boots, and sturdy boots of leather. The shirt and pants fit loosely, but the wool was comforting to his chilly skin. Oddly, he felt less vulnerable in the bulky clothes. Lacing up the boots, he enjoyed the smell and feel of the cowhide. He stomped about to test them, pleased by the squeak of leather, the manly clump of thick soles, the support to his ankles.

He had a flush of joy. His grandfather had given him boots like these. How grown up he had felt, tramping the docks beside him, their boots the same.

He remembered that he had been happy during those summers on the Cape. Everything was beautiful to him then, sea, sand, and sky, gulls, boats, and docks, fishing gear and boots. Everyone was loving and everything he did was delightful.

A sudden change of feeling, oddly distressing, now came over him. Something about the boots. He had worn the boots to school in Boston. The boys had jeered. Clodhoppers.

When had he decided that his mother's family did not measure up to his friends? When had he become so disloyal?

Feeling sad, he stowed the rest of his new clothes in his sea chest and carried his rubber boots and oilskins down to his locker in the boat room. Perhaps it was feeling sad that made him want to acknowledge the favor just done for him.

He found Will in the mess with Ross. "Thanks, Will. The clothes are fine."

Will smiled. "Now you look like one of us."

"Not yet he don't," Ross said, grinning. "Not till he loses that peachy complexion."

"I hope I never turn into an old nut like you."

As Daniel went to knock on the captain's door, he heard Ross laughing. "That's a good'un."

When the captain responded to his thanks with a smile, Daniel saw that what his mother had said was true. His uncle was looking more and more like his grandfather, with the same graying sideburns, sun-browned face, vivid blue eyes, off-center smile.

His uncle said, "Does everything fit well enough?" Even the resonant bass was his grandfather's.

"Yes, sir. Better than I expected."

His uncle's resemblance to his grandfather unsettled Daniel, gave him an odd, reluctant happiness. "Grandpa gave me boots like these when I was little. I tried to walk in step with him."

His uncle was still smiling. "You couldn't do better."

Daniel's pleasure slipped away. Was that a reproach for his failure to be what was expected? Much as he had loved his grandfather, he had no wish to be like him, or like his uncle, either. He wanted to be himself, just as he was.

His uncle seemed to sense the change in Daniel's feelings. He sighed and turned back to his papers.

"Dismissed."

NINE

PRIDE MADE DANIEL DO HIS BEST when he was called to the captain's office before drill to recite his duties and demonstrate his knots, but his hands shook so much that he thought, almost hoped, he would be told he was too slow.

But the captain nodded. "Wait in the boat room."

Ross and Abner were squabbling as usual; Will was talking quietly with Edwin and Obed, and Jon checking gear in the apparatus cart, his great dog alert beside him, as though she too were important in the drill.

Daniel waited near the door in case he had to throw up. He shivered, yet his hair was soaked with sweat. He clamped his teeth to keep them from chattering, but he could not stop the pounding of his heart. He was in anguish, not sure what he would do at the last moment. Would he dash off to Fleetport, run to the woods, fly up

63

the beach toward Pamet? Become hysterical, beg off, burst into tears? Disgrace himself?

The captain came in. The men jumped to attention.

"Number One," the captain called.

Jon saluted. "Place gun in position; load the shot . . ."

Daniel found the rest incomprehensible. Of what the others recited he understood only part: Ed's "Place shot-line box in position," Abner's "Unload buoy from cart," Obed's "Bury sand anchor."

"Daniel!" the captain barked.

Startled, Daniel stepped forward and saluted. His words came out as of their own accord. "On command of 'forward,' go to the wreck pole. On command of 'action,' climb to the crow's-nest. When the shot line is fired across the crow's-nest, take it in hand and signal to the captain to tie on the whip. Haul in the whip and fasten tail block to the pole. Fasten hawser to the pole. When breeches buoy comes out, climb in and ride down."

The captain called, "Open the doors! Man the cart."

The men grasped the hauling ropes. Daniel took the rear with the captain.

"Forward!" the captain cried. Running hard, the men dragged the cart with its rattling gear out and around the station. At the steep incline to the lower beach, they fell back on the ropes to check the cart and then dashed on with it over the sand. Trueheart ran alongside.

Fired by excitement, Daniel rushed across the beach

to the wreck pole, grasped the spikes, put one foot up, and waited for the next command.

The men ran on with the cart until the captain shouted, "Halt!" The captain pulled out his watch, gave it a glance, and cried, "Action!"

Still in the heat of the moment, Daniel went up three spikes. Then he froze, realizing that he was committed. He could not escape. Neither could he climb. Panic swept him. A ringing filled his ears. The sky went black.

He became aware of roaring breakers and the sound of men unloading gear, shoveling sand, preparing for Daniel to do his part. Daniel could not bear to be found lacking. He forced himself to step up one spike and then another. Wind chilled his damp face. His hands slipped on the cold spikes.

Suddenly he had to know how much farther there was to climb. He squinted up the wreck pole. He was not even halfway to the top.

Fighting an urge to look down, he shut his eyes and climbed on until he bumped his head on the crow's-nest. It took all the strength he could muster to pull himself onto the platform.

There he crouched against the pole—gasping, dizzy, and faint—until he remembered he had been told to watch the action. Clamping his arms around the pole, he dragged himself to his feet. He saw the men scurrying about, hauling the gun into place, setting out the tall wooden crotch that supported the breeches buoy. He saw Trueheart on the sidelines, overseeing all.

He also saw rushing clouds. The wreck pole became a mast in heavy weather, vibrating, swaying, tipping against the sky, seeming about to splinter and go crashing down.

Daniel's stomach heaved. He slipped to his knees and buried his face in his jacket. He heard the cannon boom and echo under the cliffs. Something whistled past him over the crow's-nest and thudded to the beach. Vaguely Daniel realized he had something to do, but he could do nothing.

Someone was shouting his name. But the important thing was not to let go of the pole, not to throw up.

Boots came rapidly crunching over the sand. Boots scraped the spikes. The wreck pole trembled. Someone invaded Daniel's space. Hands reached over his head and snatched the line, began hauling on a rope and slapping it into place. A pulley squealed.

"On your feet, Daniel! Get in the buoy."

"I can't."

Someone tried to pry Daniel's arms from the pole, but they were clamped. Someone pulled Daniel's head up by the hair. A fist crashed into his jaw. Light streaked across the sky. The sky went black.

Daniel was flying. Wind whipped his face. His legs felt heavy, dangling through short canvas breeches. Then his boots dragged in the sand. He was lifted out. He doubled over and threw up on the beach.

Someone cried, "Get him to the station."

Something pungent burned his nostrils. Something cold lay on his jaw.

The captain was taking his pulse. Jon was waving a strong-smelling bottle under his nose. Will, Ed, and Obed were at the foot of his bed. Trueheart's big paws clawed at his blanket. When she saw Daniel looking at her, she whimpered and slowly wagged her tail.

"Get down, girl," Jon said. "He's all right."

Daniel tested his jaw to see if it was as big as it felt.

"I'm sorry, Daniel," Will said. "Guess I nearly broke your face."

"What day is it?" Daniel asked, afraid it was time for the beach drill.

The strong-smelling bottle passed under his nose again. A glass was held to his lips and someone told him to drink. Daniel remembered that the beach drill was over. Burning with shame, he closed his eyes and turned away.

"He'll sleep now, Captain," Jon said.

"I think he's asleep already," Obed whispered.

The men trooped out. Trueheart's claws scraped the floor as she ran after them.

Drifting, Daniel heard a whisper. "Captain, got a minute?"

"Yes, Number Six?"

The voices and footsteps receded through the men's sleeping quarters and down the stairs.

TEN

WHEN DANIEL HEARD THE MEN gathering for supper, he got out of bed and went downstairs, braced for a ragging.

"Here's Danny!" Obed called. "How do you feel, Danny?"

Trueheart rushed over to explore him with sniffs. He rubbed her great head as she escorted him to the table.

"Glad to see you up, Daniel," the captain said.

Obed pulled a chair out for him. "Get some food in you, Danny. You ain't hardly ate nothing all day."

The captain offered bread. Will dished up Daniel's codfish cakes. Ed poured his milk.

Ross laughed. "Anybody'd think Six and a Half was back from the beyond."

Daniel felt that sportsmanship required him to apologize.

"Listen, men. I'm sorry I ruined the drill."

The men laughed. Ed thumped him on the back.

"What's for dessert?" Ross asked.

Obed said, "Indian pudding!" The men cheered.

Daniel felt belittled. What was so momentous to him mattered less than pudding to these men. Yet he had to admit that some of them had tried to be kind.

Daniel made up his mind not to worry about Monday's breeches buoy drill. He would find some way to get out of it when the time came, even if he had to beg the captain on his knees, even if he had to run and hide somewhere.

He slept well, awoke in good spirits, and got up to help Obed with breakfast.

Friday's drill was bandaging, splints, and resuscitation.

"Resuscitation—" Obed began.

"Is a technique to help drowning victims breathe again," Daniel said. "Will told me."

Obed beamed. "You're going to be real good at drills, Danny. You learn something quick as you hear it."

Will added, "Jon worked on a man for two hours once and brought him back after the doctor called him dead."

Daniel nodded eagerly. What they were doing today did seem quite worth learning, even useful back home.

The next day, Saturday, Daniel worked alongside the men to scrub floors, clean windows, shine brass, and polish the stove. He went on cheerfully to wash his own bedding, towels, and clothes.

After supper, Obed set himself up in the galley as

barber for the men who were going to church next day.

"This week it's Will, Ed, and me. I'll see my grandma, and Ed will see his daughters, and Will—" Obed broke off as Will came in with a towel around his neck.

"Want to come with us, Danny? Ask the captain."

Daniel decided he would like that. He'd be glad for the change, and he was curious to see Ed's daughters. Ed, Will, and Obed were the three surfmen he had begun to like.

Now he was sorry he had refused to wear an apron in the galley.

"Afraid I got spots on my only good trousers."

"I'll sponge and press them for you, Danny."

What a kind man, Daniel thought. Why had he not realized that before?

To Daniel's surprise, the captain seemed pleased to grant his request.

For the rest of the evening, Daniel had to help Obed fill and empty the tub set behind the stove for the surfmen's baths. He did not mind even that.

The next morning, Ed and Obed improved themselves for church with white shirts and neckties under their seamen's jackets. Will appeared in a suit the equal of Daniel's own, and a derby, too.

Laughing, Ross slapped his thigh. "Will, if your lady don't take a shine to you in that hat, better look elsewhere."

The sun was warm in a brilliant sky as the men set out. Daniel and Obed walked at a comfortable pace, but Will and Ed trudged swiftly up the sandy slope and were soon well ahead.

"Will can't wait to see Rachel," Obed said. "Only time he sees her now is in church. I don't blame him for missing her sore." Obed sighed. "But now she favors that other one."

"Do you know why she turned Will down?" Daniel asked. Earlier, Daniel had wondered what dark secret fault Rachel had discovered in Will. Now Daniel did not see how there could be anything wrong with the man.

"Nobody knows why she turned Will down," Obed said. "Not even Will."

They walked on in silence a while. For the first time, Daniel noticed how pretty the road was. Bayberries and Queen Anne's lace grew on either side, among shrubs and stunted pines. Farther on, through trees glowing with autumn color, he could see a blue pond with shimmering borders. A doe splashed along the shore, throwing up glints of silver.

"You'll meet my grandma," Obed said. "Ain't no finer woman on this Cape, nobody kinder, wiser, nor yet more beautiful, allowing for her years."

Ahead was the white church Daniel remembered, square clock tower topped by a circular bell tower with a high dome. As they approached, great peals set the air throbbing. Daniel felt the odd mix of joy and sadness that had moved him lately. Tolling bells, aroma of bayberry, twittering birds, sun on his neck, love for his grandparents, everything was here from the Sundays of his childhood except his grandparents themselves.

A little woman in black stepped out of a crowd at the church doors and waved her umbrella.

Obed hurried over to her. "Here's our new surfman, Grandma. Here's Danny!"

The old woman's face was nearly hidden in a deep bonnet, but Daniel could see that her chin was firm and her eyes dark and lively.

"How do you do, Mrs. Woolsey?" Daniel pulled off his hat. His impression that her bones were delicate vanished with her handshake. Her sharp eyes raked over him.

"Surfman, is it? Bitten off a mite for your years."

"Oh, Danny's keen, Grandma," Obed said. "He'll be a first-rate surfman."

Daniel was surprised and pleased to hear that. Of course it was not what he or his mother expected, but he didn't want to let that be known just then. Still, he felt a need to make some sort of response. He said, "But I have a lot to learn."

"That's all right then," Mrs. Woolsey said.

From her huge handbag she brought out a bundle and thrust it at Obed. "Time you had a new Sunday shirt. Now I have to say hello to the minister's wife." She thumped Daniel's arm. "Young man, you come visit."

Beaming, Obed watched his grandmother scurry away. "Ain't she all I said?"

"And more."

"There's Will and Ed and his daughters," Obed said. Will had his derby clamped to his heart. He looked so glum that one might think he despised the company.

Obed said, "Mighty fine-looking girls, ain't they?"

"Mighty fine," Daniel said, although their backs were turned and he couldn't see their faces. In plain gowns and shawls, one looked plump and the other thin, and neither seemed attractive enough to cause Will such anguish.

Ed gestured for Obed and Daniel to join them.

"Girls, this here is Daniel Stafford," he said. "Dan, Rachel my eldest and Fannie my younger."

Daniel swept off his hat again as Rachel turned to him. Facing him, she looked altogether different, with handsome curves, ample bust, small waist. She offered her hand and the attention of her green crystal eyes.

"How do, Dan." Her voice was warm, serene, and deep for a girl. Her smile revealed small, perfect teeth. Under her bonnet, the hair framing her face was as red-gold as Will's. Daniel could not help staring.

"And this is Fannie," Rachel said.

"How do, Dan." Grinning, Fannie used Daniel's hand like a pump, as though to bring up his wits.

Unlike Rachel, Fannie was straight as a plank. Her eyes were bright agate and her dark hair silky, but her teeth looked too broad in her narrow face.

Daniel liked the hearty younger sister at once, but it was at the elder that he kept stealing glimpses.

Abruptly Will said, "Rachel, how's your aunt?" He

gave Rachel a swift glance, then stared at the buttons on his vest.

Rachel looked at the church door instead of at Will. "She's acting poorly today."

"Acting is right," Fannie said. "People shouldn't ask how Aunt Violet is. It only makes her act worse."

"You mustn't rebuke Will for his courtesy," Rachel said.

"Will pays me no mind, do you, Will?" Fannie said. "And neither does Aunt Violet, so much the worse for her."

Fannie turned to grin at Obed. "Tell your grandma we'll come to supper on your next day off, if you'll make us a cranberry pie."

Obed flushed with pleasure. "That I will, Fannie."

"Fannie, you are a scandal today," Rachel said. "We mustn't invite ourselves to Obed's. Ask them to us."

"We won't have such a good supper if they come to us."

Obed laughed and so did Daniel, but Will frowned. Daniel saw that he was frowning at the man coming toward them. The man was young, well-dressed, and oddly handsome, with dark wavy hair and a chalky complexion, but his eyes were such a pale gray they were hardly visible. He went to Rachel, spoke in her ear, and offered his arm.

"Aren't the rest of us worth greeting, Percy?" Ed asked.

"How do, sir. Fannie. Obed." Instead of nods, Percy

74

offered backward jerks of his head. "And you, William, no less." The smile he gave Will was not pleasant. His gaze fell on Daniel. "And this?"

"Daniel Stafford," Ed said. "Dan, this is Percy Yates."

"Stafford?" Percy said, as though testing the name.

Daniel glared at him. "Of the Boston Staffords."

"And isn't it a dandy little gentleman!" said Percy.

"Gentleman enough to take his hat off before ladies." Daniel was pleased to see color rise in the man's pale face.

Fannie laughed. Will showed his first smile of the day, but it fell when Percy said to Rachel, "Shall we go in?"

When they were gone, Daniel asked, "Who is that fellow?"

"Son of Captain Yates," Edwin said.

"Richest man in Fleetport," Fannie said. "He never lets anybody forget it."

Percy led Rachel to a pew where there was room only for the two of them. Edwin, Fannie, and Will went on to the pew ahead. Obed and Daniel sat with Obed's grandmother, behind and to the side of Rachel. There Daniel found that he could admire Rachel's profile freely. While he looked at her, he was surprised to see that she kept glancing at Will.

The minister climbed to the pulpit and opened his Bible.

"Dear brothers and sisters," he said. "We come to another change of season. For some it is the culmination of the year, with harvest and Thanksgiving followed by rest from the labors of field and sea." He paused.

"For others a season of labor begins, arduous, perilous labor with few earthly rewards. Yet that labor more closely follows the teachings of our Lord than any other labor does in our time.

"At his final supper with his disciples, Jesus said, 'A new commandment I give unto you, that ye love one another.'"

Daniel saw Rachel glance at Will again. She looked wistful, even sad.

The minister went on, "And Jesus said, 'Greater love hath no man than this, that he lay down his life for his friends.' Most of us are never asked to make such a terrible sacrifice. How many would do it? Yet there are men among us, husbands, sons, fathers, brothers, who stand ready at any moment to lay down their lives, not just for friends, but for strangers."

The minister paused. "My brothers and sisters, I feel humble before them."

Obed's grandmother looked at Obed, her sharp eyes gone mellow. Fannie smiled at her father and then turned to grin at Daniel. Daniel smiled back because he liked her, but he felt it was not right to accept any tribute. He was not and could not be a real surfman. His mother had decreed it. At that moment he was resentful.

He glanced at Rachel. She was looking at Will again, her head fallen to the side, as though she were weary.

76

She is thinking about Will all the time, Daniel thought.

Now he saw that her eyes were glistening. She touched the corners discreetly with a handkerchief. Daniel thought, She loves him, that's what it is. She loves him as much as he loves her.

ELEVEN

WHEN DANIEL, WILL, AND OBED started back to the station after church, Ed was not with them.

"Went home with Rachel," Will explained morosely. "He's on leave until tomorrow morning."

"We all get a night off every eight days," Obed said.

While Obed talked about his night off next Wednesday and what he would cook for the girls, Will stared at his shoes, and Daniel puzzled over the situation between him and Rachel.

Obviously Daniel could not tell Will what he had discovered about Rachel's feelings, because for whatever reason, she did not want Will to know.

Hoping to make Will feel better, Daniel said in a loud voice, "I can't stand that fellow Percy. What an ass!"

When he saw that Will had perked up, Daniel went on. "I don't think Rachel likes Percy much. All the time

78

he was whispering to her in church she looked at—other people."

"Then, it's terrible if she's set on marrying him," Obed said. "She doesn't have to marry yet; she's only eighteen."

After dinner, some of the men had free time. Abner challenged Obed to a game of tiddlywinks. Ross read the *Chatham Monitor.* Will stared blankly at an open book on his lap. Daniel watched the tiddlywinks game.

Between clouds of pipe smoke, Ross said, "Listen to this. 'Monday instant the old lighthouse in Chatham was scheduled to plunge over the bank into the sea. People gathered for the show, but it did not come off and the party was postponed.'"

Abner laughed but Obed looked distressed. "My grandma says more of that bank is washed away every storm. The keeper's been measuring the bank ever since the hurricane of '70 and writing to the government but they don't answer him nothing. He goes on doing his duty by that light, never knowing when it will be swept away and him along with it."

Abner's tiddlywink missed the cup. "Duty! All he does is trim wicks and polish lenses. That ain't nothing compared to the duty of a surfman."

Ross said, "And he gets more pay for it. I say let him run out and measure the bank, do something to earn his money."

Abner missed the cup again. He glared at Daniel. "Don't stand there. You're spoiling my aim."

Daniel strolled over to look at the bookshelves. He

found only sermons, seamanship, mathematics, and geography.

The argument went on, Obed saying how much harder the surfman's job would be without lighthouses. When Abner's tiddlywink fell into the cup, he praised the government for its free lighthouse service to ships of all nations.

"It ain't free," Ross said. "It comes out of our taxes."

Abner laughed. "You'd deprive the government of a right smart revenue if you'd give up tobacco."

Daniel decided to try to distract Will from his worries.

"These books look pretty dull. Why didn't you men choose something more interesting?"

Will sighed. "We didn't choose them. They're on loan from the Seamen's Friend Society." He added despondently, "They try to send what's useful and uplifting."

Daniel lowered his voice. "It seems to me most of the men here don't care for what's uplifting. They'd rather argue, joke, and play silly games."

"Just trying to forget their loneliness and family problems and all the tragedy they see every season."

Daniel regretted his criticism. He felt a need to make amends. "Will, I'm sorry for how I've behaved here. I was forced to come here, you know, and give up everything at home. I hated being here. I even thought of running away."

Will smiled. "I know, but you didn't. You'll make a surfman, Daniel."

Hadn't Obed said something like that to his grandmother? Daniel wondered if it could be true.

"Feel like helping me study signal flags?" he asked.

"Glad to!"

At last Daniel had said something to distract Will.

At eight o'clock Daniel went to his locker to get his slickers and rubber boots for his first patrol. He looked forward to wearing them. They now seemed the garb of heroes.

To his disappointment, Obed said, "You won't need those tonight, Danny." He gave Daniel three rods. "Hang these on your belt. They're Coston lights, for signaling vessels in trouble that we're coming to the rescue."

The lights seemed even more heroic than the slickers and boots. Thrilled, Daniel said, "Will we need them tonight?"

"We never know."

Daniel picked up his lantern and followed Obed.

There was no need for lanterns. Enormous stars seemed to hang within reach of Daniel's fingers. The Milky Way was like a bridge of snow spanning ocean, earth, and sky, dense enough to bear a sleigh. Daniel had forgotten how a night sky could look, away from city lights. Staring up, circling, he felt as though he were spinning on a rock in timeless space.

Obed laughed. "I feel like that, sometimes, when the sky is uncommon clear. It's so mysterious and beautiful it's more than a man can say." He gave Daniel a brotherly slap on the back. Daniel felt a rush of warmth for the big man.

They walked on hard-packed sand where the tide had left firm footing. Breakers rumbled in from the black sea, crashed, and sent thunder echoing alongshore. Surf rushed up to the beach again and again and dragged a catch of stranded sea creatures and shells back to the ocean. A spire of light swung up over the cliffs and circled the sky.

"The Highland Light," Obed said. "Been shining out from the tip of the Cape for more'n eighty year, no light anywhere more powerful. In clear weather, she can be seen from forty-five mile off."

"Ross and Abner seem angry that lighthouse keepers get more pay than surfmen," Daniel said.

"They're only funning. We don't begrudge the keepers nothing. The lights make our work easier. They have led many a vessel to safe harbor."

The heavy Obed turned out to be a fast, nimble walker. Crunching along behind him, Daniel tried to keep an eye out for things he dreaded to step on, scuttling things, stranded jellyfish, creatures in shells, things both living and dead.

Obed laughed. "No point going on patrol if you keep eyeing your boots, Danny. There's something you ought to take account of, that schooner beyond the shoals."

Daniel could barely make out a red light bobbing under faintly glimmering sails.

"Is she in trouble?" he asked, excited.

"No, she's moving easy toward Provincetown. But we need to know she's out there, just the same."

This was no mere stroll along the shore. By now Daniel was breathing hard. "What's it like patrolling in a storm?"

"It ain't nothing you'd enjoy like this. The sand whips up all around and cuts your skin to shreds. You can hold a shingle to your face but it don't help much. In a bad'un you can't see nothing. Waves break at the dunes and you have to walk along the top. Sometimes the dunes cave in. You have to take care you don't go down with them and get swept to sea."

Obed glanced at him. "But never you mind, Danny. It ain't likely the captain will send you out in such weather."

"Have you lifesavers always patrolled like this?"

"Just since '72 when the stations was built. Some of us volunteered before then, but we had no regular patrols. We had to know the coast like our own back-yard, just the same, because most wrecks happen just offshore. And we had to know how to handle a boat in the surf. It ain't the same as at sea. From shipboard, you can't judge breakers, surf, or undertow. It don't even look dangerous. But if seamen try to come ashore in their boats they're like to capsize. It's safer for them to wait to be rescued, even if their vessel is cracking up."

Obed was as talkative as usual, but Daniel now realized that he had been wrong to think what Obed said was idle chatter. Daniel's respect for the man was growing, along with his affection.

Obed pointed out vessels showing red lights as they went north or green as they went south, and fishing schooners at anchor two or three miles offshore, with lanterns high on their masts.

"What happens if there's a wreck in summer when the captain is on duty by himself?" Daniel asked.

"We surfmen are called out. We get extra pay for that, three dollars a day, ten if we save a life."

"Ten dollars? Is that all they think a life is worth?"

"It's fair and more. It's a week's pay."

The men risk their lives for ten dollars a week, Daniel thought. But as Obed had told him earlier, they did not do it just for the money.

Up ahead, stark against the silver beach, Daniel saw what looked like the skeleton of a great animal. "Is that a wreck?"

"Yes, a brigantine, seems like, from the way she was masted. Been there since before stations was built. She's buried now and again when the sand shifts, but she always comes up."

Daniel walked around the mammoth shell, looking at the ribs and timbers and the weird shadows they threw on the beach in the moonlight. "Pirate ship?"

"Might be. But you won't find no treasure. She was swept clean long ago by wreckers. Nary a spike left."

They trudged on. Daniel did not like to admit it, but he was tired. "How much farther do we go?"

"That's halfway house up ahead, where we meet the surfman from Pamet River. He'll be along."

Halfway house was a shingled hut set well back from the ocean, with a narrow door facing south. Obed lit his lantern and set it on a table. Daniel sank into a chair.

The hut held another chair, a chest, and a small stove with firewood stacked nearby. A row of Coston lights hung on the wall beside a barometer and a shelf of cans and jugs.

"That's hardtack and water for shipwrecked people who can't get to a station. We store blankets here, too."

The door swung open and a dark, stocky man in a seaman's jacket came in. He offered his hand to Daniel.

"Is this the young feller you got taking charge at Perkins Hollow?"

"Daniel Stafford," Obed said. "Fortune Smith, Danny."

Fortune grinned at Daniel. "You going to be on hand when we shame your crew in the beach-drill contest?"

"When we shame you, more likely," Daniel said.

The man laughed and gave him a slap on the arm.

Obed and Fortune showed Daniel their metal checks, which were like small badges with the surfman's number and name of his station.

Fortune said, "We trade these to prove we met and didn't stop in town for a pint."

"He's funning, Danny," Obed said.

When they parted with the Pamet River surfman, Daniel asked, "Is Fortune really his name?"

"It's Fortunato. Portuguese. Smith is from the captain of the whaler he signed on with as a lad. Lots of Portuguese did that. Lots of them stay on here after they been to sea. They know a good thing."

On the way back to their station, Obed told Daniel that to fire the Coston light, he must strike the bottom of the holder to drive the spike into the cartridge. Obed said it would brighten the sky with a great red flare and signal to ships in distress that help was coming.

Daniel had found the patrol so interesting and tiring that he forgot what he wanted to ask Obed until they were nearly back to the station. He wasn't sure how he was going to bring it up, but then a way occurred to him naturally.

"I'm starving. Sure could do with some of your cranberry pie, just now."

"I'll make one for you, first chance I get."

"Wish I could be there when you make it for the girls." Daniel sighed. "Wish I had leave, same as you. Wish I had someplace to go."

Obed looked surprised. "Would you like to come home with me?"

"More than anything! But I don't know if the captain would let me go, unless somebody spoke for me."

"I'll speak for you, Danny. Certain I will!"

TWELVE

DANIEL WAS NOW GETTING used to rising early, dressing quickly, and taking his turn to wash at the pump. On Monday, however, he got up reluctantly, not just because he was tired after last night's patrol, but because the beach drill would be held again today. His first climb up the wreck pole was dreadful to remember. He couldn't hope even to do that well again. Though ashamed, he went to the captain's door to plead his case. He was about to knock when Obed came up.

"He's doing reports, Danny. Best not to bother him."

Daniel's other idea was to disappear, but he couldn't do that, either, because Obed took his arm and led him toward the boat room. "You all right? You hardly ate any breakfast."

Trying to hide his trembling, Daniel said, "I'm fine."

They went on to the boat room. The captain

appeared. Automatically, Daniel snapped to attention. The captain said, "Number Six, help bury the sand anchor, then go to the wreck pole as victim. Daniel, take orders from Number Five."

There was not a question, not a raised eyebrow from the men. Daniel was flooded with relief and euphoria.

The surfmen barked out their duties. Daniel cried, "Take orders from Obed—Number Five, sir!"

Obed flung open the doors. The men jumped to their places on the hauling ropes. The captain shouted, "Forward!"

Daniel and Trueheart rushed out behind the rumbling cart. Down the slope they all went and off along the shore until the captain shouted, "Halt!" Trueheart ran over to the dunes and sat up in strict attention.

The captain took out his watch. "Action!"

The surfmen scampered about in what seemed frenzied haste, unloading the cart, setting up the cannon, placing the shot line. Daniel looked on, bewildered.

"Danny!" Obed called. "Help dig for the sand anchor."

Obed and Will had already started a trench. Daniel grabbed a shovel and set to work, madly scattering sand.

Ross gave a shout of laughter. "A dog covering his—"

"Mind your own job, Ross!" Will cried.

Obed said, "Danny, pile the sand up here. We need it for burying the anchor."

The trench finished, Will dashed off to the wreck pole. Watching Will climb, admiring his ease and speed, Daniel tripped over the tackle of the tall wooden crotch that the men were setting up to support the breeches buoy.

Ross grinned. "If you don't beat all for clumsy!"

The cannon fired the shot line out to Will. The men lined up to haul out the hawser with the breeches buoy attached. Daniel took Will's place, but when he tried to pull in unison with the men, he slipped in the sand and fell against Obed.

Ross laughed. "Leave it before you hurt yourself again!"

Will came flying down in the breeches buoy. The captain and Jon hurried over to help him get out. Trueheart ran up wagging joyfully, as though at a real rescue.

The captain checked his watch. "Five minutes, fifteen seconds."

"Then we still haven't qualified," Abner said.

"We'll make it next time," Will said.

Ross grinned at Daniel. "Certain we will, if we let Trueheart do for Six and a Half."

Daniel flared up. "I've had enough of you, Ross!" He sprang into the boxing stance he and his friends had learned at the gymnasium, head erect and haughty, left fist raised above right. "Put up your dukes!"

Ross roared with laughter. Daniel feinted with his left and crossed with his right, but Ross shoved his fist aside and held him off with one big hand to the chest. Daniel was whipping air.

Abner laughed in great brays. The captain looked on impassively. The other men stood around, grinning.

Ross said, "My, my! The banty cock's got into a huff."

"Damn you!" Daniel cried. "Fight like a man!"

Huge arms pinned Daniel from behind. "Stop, Danny!" Obed cried. "He's only funning."

Helpless in Obed's vise, Daniel had to relent.

Jon said, "Get to work, men!"

As ordered by Obed, Daniel helped wipe down the hawser and stow the apparatus. Trudging after the cart over the beach back to the station, Daniel felt a double humiliation. He had failed again. He had made a fool of himself.

He began to wonder why he had been taken off the wreck pole. It was not like the captain to let anybody escape his assigned duty. Daniel followed the captain to his office.

"Speak to you, sir?"

"Yes. Come in." The captain was at his desk. Daniel closed the door and stood before him.

"Sir, I want to know why you took me off the wreck pole."

The captain looked at him thoughtfully, tapping a stack of papers with a pencil in his big fist.

Daniel said, "I know we are never to question orders, sir, but this is different, sir."

"Do you want the job back?"

Daniel had not expected to hear that. Pride made him want to say yes, but dread prevented it. "Well, sir, I . . ."

"Never mind, Daniel. I am not going to say you must."

Daniel burned to know if the captain suspected his secret. "Why not, sir?"

The captain rose, went to his window, and looked out at the breakers. "Will asked to replace you. He said he didn't see how you climbed that pole the first time. He'd recognized your problem when he saw you struggling to get down the cliff from the watch house."

Daniel's face caught fire with shame.

"Will thinks you were mighty brave, trying to do your duty on the wreck pole just the same. So do I. I understand that phobia, Daniel. I had it myself, once."

"You, sir!"

The captain nodded. "I did, until your grandfather helped me. Shall I try to help you, Daniel?"

"Oh, no, sir, I wouldn't take you from your work." Actually, Daniel did not want to be shamed before his uncle any more, even though his uncle appeared sympathetic.

"As you wish. You are not obliged."

After supper that night, Daniel wrote to his mother that things were going better for him, some of the men were nice, the food was good. Then he realized that if he said things were better, his perceptive mother would realize that things had not been so good earlier. He tore up the letter and wrote cheerfully about going on leave soon with Obed.

To Arthur, he wrote at length about his gratitude to Will. "Even though he's so miserable himself, he took the trouble to help me. I wish I could do something for him. If only I could find out what's wrong between him and Rachel."

Daniel could hardly wait for boat drill on Tuesday.

He meant to redeem himself, astonish them all, Ross in particular, with his skill as an oarsman.

He approached Jon eagerly. "Which oar will I pull, sir?"

"You don't row, Daniel. You're to help launch the boat and observe the drill from shore."

"I don't need to observe! I know all about rowing."

"Give Daniel his orders, Number Five," Jon said. He went on to the boat room with Trueheart dashing after him.

"I can row!" Daniel cried to Obed. "I've been training for a regatta."

Obed's mild face went stony. "We never argue. We obey and that's all. Do you understand?"

Daniel was so surprised by the change in Obed that he could only stammer, "Yes, sir."

"When we get the boat to the surf, you will stand by the captain at the stern. At command to launch, you will help get the boat out and keep it from broaching. Once we're aboard, you fall back. Watch us row out past the breakers, capsize, and right the boat."

"You're going to dump yourselves into the sea?" Daniel's indignation at not being allowed to row began to wane.

"Yes, that's part of every boat drill. When we come in, you will meet us and help get the boat up the beach."

Obed became himself again. "You'll have a chance with the oars one day, Danny, certain you will."

As something to be hauled, Daniel found the surfboat on its carriage formidable, towering over all their heads, even Jon's. But the men lined up on the hauling ropes and on command rushed the great boat out through the doors, down the ramp, around the station, and off to the beach as fast as they had pulled the cart. Daniel followed and Trueheart ran alongside, her tail thrashing with excitement.

The men ran alongshore until the captain called, "Stop!" They sped the boat to the surf, lifted it off its carriage, and got the carriage back up on the beach. They took life belts from the boat and strapped them on. The captain put the steering oar in place. The surf-men grasped the gunwales on either side of the boat and waited tensely.

Daniel took his place at the stern beside the captain. As something on which to launch a boat, the ocean was different from what Daniel had known as a child, playing in the surf. Great mounds of water roared in toward the beach, crested, tumbled over, and came one after another in wild surges of power before turning into foam.

The captain was studying the sea so intently that Daniel wondered if he were doubtful about launching today.

"Rough, isn't it, sir?"

"Not bad."

"What are we waiting for?"

"The slatch." The captain did not break his attention. "Slack water followed by a backwash to sea, usually the seventh wave after the biggest."

Now Daniel saw that waves were not all the same size. Big ones rolled in one after another, then a small one followed and crested. The captain shouted, "Now!"

The men rushed the boat into the sea, with Daniel and the captain shoving from the stern. They all ran out waist deep. As each section of the boat swept free, a man scrambled aboard facing the stern and wrestled his oar into place.

The sea rose up and took the boat. The captain leaped in over the stern and seized the long steering oar.

"Pull!" he cried. "Pull!"

The boat lunged through the water. Daniel fell back. He slipped in the pushing waves but kept his eyes riveted on the rowers, their huge arms and shoulders pulling in mighty strokes as they concentrated on the captain.

The captain was standing upright at his oar in the stern. Foam crashed over his back. Spray flew high overhead. Daniel saw him steer away from the biggest waves until they broke, but when one came that he could not avoid, he called for speed and sent the boat head on. A great sea broke over the bow and drenched the men. They did not falter or even wince.

Daniel was astounded by the surfmen's skill, power, and daring, and by the beauty of the white surfboat flying through glittering spray. He cheered, prancing, sloshing, and waving. A roaring mountain of sea came at him, ready to break over him. He saw it just in time, turned, and plunged toward shore.

The dog ran up and down the beach barking exuberantly as Daniel came splashing through the surf. She rushed at him, tail pumping madly, and nuzzled her cold nose into his hand.

"So you think I'm all right after all, do you, old girl?" Daniel laughed, roughing up her shaggy head.

Together they patrolled the beach, watching the surfboat. Out past the breakers, the boat capsized. The men bobbed in the sea. The dog stiffened and stared out intently. She did not relax until the boat was righted and the crew back at their oars.

"Ready to go to the rescue, right, old girl?" Daniel asked. He told her she was a noble dog.

Coming back with the boat looked even more hazardous than launching. The boat flew in ahead of a great swell, the captain standing in the stern, spray breaking around him.

Daniel felt a surge of joy at the sight of him. He remembered what old Barnaby Duff had told him on the train. "That's the finest man I ever expect to meet this life." Daniel thought, Wouldn't Grandpa be proud of him!

Any oarsman, even the athletes of Daniel's club, would be impressed by this crew. The rowing Daniel and his friends did on a calm river, with nothing to think about but stroke and speed, was mere play compared to the efforts of these mighty oarsmen, which were not for sport, but in preparation to save lives.

It was no small thing to be a surfman, Daniel decided. It would be no small thing to be counted as one among them.

THIRTEEN

ON WEDNESDAY DANIEL AWOKE joyfully, looking forward to the day off with Obed and supper with Rachel and Fannie.

But first came signal-flag drill. With Will's help, Daniel had worked hard to learn the signals, and he was eager for some acknowledgment of his progress, as he would have had in school. As usual, however, Jon passed over all correct answers. Will and Obed nodded at Daniel's snappy responses. Ross grinned at him and whispered, "Showoff."

Carrying a bundle for overnight, Daniel set out with Obed on the sandy road through the woods and past the lake. Birds chirped; insects buzzed. The air was sweet with the smell of wildflowers and berries. The sun was warm, the breeze cool. Daniel thought he had never known a more perfect day.

They turned off on a rambling lane. Obed said,

"This was a path made by the Pamet Indians when it was all forest here. They'd walk around a tree rather than cut a road; that's why the lane's so crooked. Later the settlers just used what they found. Pretty, though, ain't it?"

"Very pretty."

"That Fannie, she's found Pamet arrowheads and tomahawks plenty. She's a good'un for finding things."

"You never say much about Rachel. Don't you like her?"

"Oh, I like them both the same. 'Course, they ain't the same. Rachel stays mostly to home with their Aunt Violet. Fannie runs about free as a boy, rowing, fishing, trapping. Very jolly girl."

"Will their aunt be coming to supper tonight?"

"Not likely, her being so poorly."

"What's wrong with her? Is she sick or old or what?"

"Not old, though she looks it. She's . . ." Obed paused. He appeared to see something of interest growing beside the lane. "This here is bayberry. My grandma makes candles from bayberry, and a good smell they have, too."

"What were you going to say about Aunt Violet, Obed?"

Obed said, "Here we are!"

The cottage had a white clapboard front, a great stone chimney, and a roof that hung low over windows with small shining panes. A path of crushed shells led through a patch of wildflowers to the door.

Obed's grandmother rushed out to greet them.

When Obed went off to the kitchen, his grandmother said, "Danny, come visit with me a spell, like proper company."

She took him to the parlor where small crackling flames lit up the huge fireplace. She gave him a stool, sat opposite in a rocking chair, and fixed him with glittering eyes.

"Now tell me your news."

Daniel wasn't sure what she'd like to hear, but he tried to think of something. "Well, I was good in signal-flag drill this morning. For a change. I've been terrible in everything else."

"Good."

"Good?"

"To admit that. It means you will do better."

Obed's grandmother led Daniel on to talk about the drills and the contest with the Pamet River surfmen that lay ahead. He was soon even confessing his fear of heights.

"Will's playing victim in my place. But I can't do his job as well as he does, not in time for the contest, anyway."

"Then your duty is clear. You must be victim."

Daniel felt as though a sandbag had fallen on his chest. Mrs. Woolsey looked at him closely, leaned forward, and clamped a strong hand on his wrist. "You can do it."

Daniel moaned. "Oh, I don't think so."

"Shall I tell you what I've learned in this life? Anyone can do most anything, if he sets his mind to it.

Listen. Obed was so afraid of school that he threw up every morning. He never complained, but I found out that the other children tormented him. He was different, you see, big and slow. You wouldn't notice that now, of course."

"Of course not! Not at all."

"But we knew our duty, his to go and mine to send him. And we found that he could learn, though it took him longer than most. I was worried about what he could do in life, but you see, he found his place."

Daniel had to scrub his eyes because something made them sting. He thought he saw Mrs. Woolsey's firm lips tremble.

She stood up. "That's enough visiting. Now you must be at home. Come see my chamber and the rest of the house."

Daniel followed to her room across the hall. There everything was what might be expected, poster bed, rocking chair, sewing basket. But under the window stood a table littered with wood chips, tools, and paints. On a shelf was a row of duck decoys in various stages. The finished ducks had bright eyes and finely drawn feathers.

Mrs. Woolsey said, "I make these for the pleasure. And to bring in a little extra from summer visitors."

"I never saw any that looked so real," Daniel said.

Mrs. Woolsey led him to the back of the house, which was kitchen, dining, and living room in one. It was bright with sunshine and color, orange and blue on curtains and pottery, blue and green in spatters on the wide floorboards. A delicious smell of spices hung in the air from Obed's cooking.

Obed's grandmother opened a narrow door to a flight of stairs and led Daniel to a room under the roof. There the great chimney rose through one end, the rafters were black with age, and the windows were small, but the place was cozy, with rugs on the floor and patchwork quilts on two beds.

"Obed's room. Yours, too, whenever you come to town."

As they started back down, a knock came at the door. Obed reached the door first. Daniel had told himself that Rachel could not be as beautiful as he remembered, but her red-gold hair seemed even glossier, her eyes more luminous green.

She gave Mrs. Woolsey something in a basket. "Cookies."

"Not as good as Obed's," Fannie said. She thumped Daniel on the arm. "Glad you came, Dan!"

Rachel said, "How nice to see you again, Daniel!"

Mrs. Woolsey insisted on a visit in the parlor with all the company while Obed went back to the kitchen.

Rachel said, "Thanks for the broth for Aunt Violet. It did her wonders of good."

"It would have done her more wonders to come with us."

"Fannie, please don't start that again."

"She didn't even want you to come. She wants you with her all the time, listening to her complaints and who knows what. You should put a stop to it and give

100

yourself some freedom before you start doing for a husband."

"Yes," Daniel blurted. "A girl needs time before she marries, to be sure she has the right man, someone who's settled in a good job, ready for responsibilities. Like Will Ryder. A girl couldn't find a better man than Will Ryder."

Rachel took up a cushion and examined the embroidery. "Did you do this, Mrs. Woolsey? It's beautiful."

At supper, Rachel began a stream of compliments about Obed's oyster stew, baked cucumbers, roasted potatoes, and especially his cranberry pie. Daniel kept trying but found it impossible to turn the conversation back to Will.

After supper, Obed sent Daniel and the ladies to the parlor while he cleared up. Rachel talked about needlework, allowing no interruption. Not long after Obed joined them, she said they had to get back to Aunt Violet.

"I don't see why," Fannie said. "She took to her bed before we got out the door." But Rachel insisted.

Obed offered to walk them home. He led the way, with Rachel and a lantern. Fannie held Daniel back.

"Listen, Dan, any goose could see what you were up to, praising Will." Fannie laughed. "But you are absolutely right. If only Rachel would listen. I don't understand her. She and Will used to be such good friends."

"How can she prefer that Percy!" Daniel said.

"She knows what a conceited oaf Percy is. But I say

he's worse than conceited. He's cruel and selfish underneath those airs of his, and he'd make her wretched if she married him. I've told her so, but she says she knows what she's doing."

They sighed together and went along in silence until Fannie said, "That's our house up ahead."

The day was over and all Daniel's pleasure in it gone.

But then Fannie brightened things for him. "Come home with Father on your next day off! We'll go fishing. Nothing ever seems so bad when you can catch a fat pickerel."

FOURTEEN

DANIEL'S ANXIETY OVER THE BEACH DRILL was renewed by what Obed's grandmother had said about duty. At the next drill, however, he gave himself another chance in Will's place. But he was so nervous trying to keep up that he stumbled again and snarled a line. Ross laughed at him so much that Daniel felt anything would be better than working with such a fiend.

Meanwhile, Daniel had not forgotten Will's problem. He wanted to talk to Will in private, hoping to hear his view of what had happened between him and Rachel. At last a chance came on Sunday night at the start of new assignments, when he set out on patrol with Will.

Shadows of the dunes had melted away in the dusk. The sky was dark pearl, the moon a sliver behind drifting clouds. The breakers were subdued and the surf quietly swishing.

Will walked ahead, keeping his eyes to sea, but he slumped and sighed. Daniel was silent until the sky and the beach grew darker and Will stopped to light their lanterns.

"I went home with Obed for my day off," Daniel said.

"So I heard," Will said morosely.

"Rachel and Fannie were there. We talked about you."

"But more about Percy, I reckon."

With the lanterns lit, they walked on.

Daniel said, "Rachel didn't say a word about him, but Fannie said plenty. She has a very low opinion of that oaf."

"It's what Rachel thinks that counts."

"Fannie said you and Rachel were best friends, once," Daniel ventured. "She can't understand what happened."

"Neither can I," Will said. "I thought we had an agreement. Maybe I took her for granted."

"You wouldn't do that."

"When I joined the service, I told her how proud I was to be working with her father, doing something important. She said she was happy for me. I asked if I could speak to her father, but she said wait, see how it goes, and she'd give me her answer when the season was over. I thought she wanted me to prove myself."

"Wasn't that it?" Daniel asked.

"I guess not. I worked hard and she was friendly all the while, asking how I was doing and how I felt about it. Then last spring when I reenlisted, she said we could never marry. She had a strange set look on her face and told me Percy had asked to call. Since then she's hardly spoken to me, won't even set eyes on me if she can help it."

"But she doesn't see Percy often. He's away at Harvard."

"It's his last year. Then he goes to New York to take up maritime law."

"Good. You'll be rid of him."

"Daniel, I'm afraid he means to take Rachel with him, and her aunt as well."

On Monday, Daniel tried to do Will's job in the beach drill again but he was no better, and the crew failed to qualify.

On Tuesday, eager to redeem himself, Daniel asked the captain to let him row in the boat drill. He gave every argument he could think of, his rowing experience, his swimming skill, the fact that he knew just what to expect.

The captain said, "Don't underestimate the assignment you have. No duty is more important in a rescue than that of the surfman on the beach. Not only does he help get the boat out and back, but he must build a fire and stand ready to help victims. The men who go out often come back so exhausted and frozen they need help themselves."

"Even if I never go to a rescue, sir, I want to learn boat drill."

The captain said, "Dismissed."

In the boat room, with the men dressed in oilskins and boots ready to go, the captain said, "Obed will take shore duty today. Daniel will row in his place."

Running with the crew, helping to pull the surfboat over the sand, Daniel was so exhilarated that he hardly noticed the cold and low-hanging mist. When the men got the boat off the carriage and its nose to the surf, Obed showed Daniel the thwart he would take and helped him into a cork life belt. Trueheart looked on, wagging as though giving her approval.

Daniel took hold of the gunwale. With the command to launch, he and the crew rushed the boat into the surf. When his section of the boat rode free, Daniel scrambled aboard. The captain came in over the stern and took the steering oar.

"Pull!" the captain cried.

Elated, Daniel bent to the work, matching stroke for stroke with the men, ignoring the sting of spray in his face.

"Big one ahead!" the captain shouted. "Pull!"

A flood of sea poured over the crew. Daniel was shocked. How cold seawater was, how heavy! Shivering, he lost the stroke, had a glimmer of self-doubt, but pulled on.

Daniel knew that the men rowed for half an hour. He had thought that would be easy, but soon his back was aching, his legs were trembling, and his hands seemed frozen to the oar.

Out past broken water, it was suddenly easier to row. Daniel's oar slipped and skimmed the surface. He would have fallen on his back if Will had not reached up to steady him.

He wanted to explain how it had happened, but Ross said, "Save your breath."

The captain called, "Make ready to capsize! Daniel, stay close to the boat. We'll right her soon enough."

Suddenly Daniel was floundering in heavy, icy sea. The waves seemed mountainous. His life belt held him afloat, but salt water spilled into his mouth and stung his nose and throat. Choking, he tried to keep his face up. Another wave washed over him, rushed into his ears and eyes. A roaring filled his head. He could make out neither boat nor shore, but only sea and mist all around.

The current was dragging him, but he could not tell whether to the beach or out to sea. He did not know which way to swim. In the terrible cold, he grew weak.

Faintly, he heard someone calling, but the voice seemed to be coming from nowhere. His bewilderment turned to fear. Worse, he was ashamed. He would not scream for help.

Another wave battered his face and then another. His lungs went raw with the pain of coughing. He saw his mother with ringlets at her ears, Mrs. O'Till wagging a finger at him, Rachel with sad eyes and smiling lips, Arthur running beside him as he wobbled, wobbled on his bicycle. He went dizzy with the wobbling.

A huge arm fell across his chest and clamped on.

"Breathe easy, son. You're all right."

His body went floating through the sea. Hands reached down for him and pulled him into the surfboat.

He doubled over, gasping and retching.

"Why didn't you sing out?" someone said. "We didn't know where to look for you."

"Good thing you were coughing," someone else said.

"Thought you'd swim ashore, did you?" Daniel knew that laughing voice. "Had enough rowing?"

Daniel flared with anger at Ross, even at the man, whoever it was, that had rescued him and humiliated him.

"All right, men, let's go in," the captain said. "Daniel, rest easy there on the bottom."

"No, sir! No, sir!" Daniel spluttered. "I can row."

He scrambled to his thwart and took his oar.

"Good man," Edwin said.

Daniel set his jaw and pulled with all his strength. As they approached broken water again, Jon called, "What say, Captain, shall we turn about?"

Daniel had learned that when the sea was very heavy it was safest to go in stern first. To him, these waves looked gigantic, boat-crushing, but the captain spoke easily. "No need, she'll make it."

The boat ran with the waves. The stern flew up and the bow went down in a rocking motion that made Daniel queasy.

"Ready to back oars for a big one!" the captain shouted.

Daniel knew the command would be to row in the opposite direction to steady the boat against a big oncoming wave and keep it from being overtaken and thrown end over end. Daniel waited tensely for the order.

"Back oars!" Daniel was not fast enough. His oar crashed against the one in front of him.

"Ship your oar!" the captain shouted at him. Daniel pulled in the oar and stowed it. He clutched the gunwale, eyes shut tight, and tried to keep from throwing up.

"Ship oars!"

Oars clattered into the boat as it sped through shallow water. The men leaped out. Daniel climbed over the side. Holding the gunwale, trying to help guide and steady the boat through water up to his waist, he struggled to stay on his feet. Obed dashed out to help pull the boat up on the beach.

Daniel's legs were trembling. His boots slipped on the wet sand. His knees buckled. He went down and his right ankle twisted under him. Pain shot up his leg.

Edwin pulled him up on one leg. Pain throbbed through his injured leg and dangling foot. Trueheart ran to him and touched his injured ankle with her nose, whining in sympathy.

Daniel was soaked to the skin and shaking.

Ross grinned. "Let that salt water dry up on you and you won't catch cold."

"Oh, dry up yourself!" Daniel said, teeth chattering. Ross laughed.

"Ross, you and Ed get him to the station," the captain ordered. "The rest of us will finish here."

Daniel hobbled between them while Trueheart ran alongside, looking up at him with anxious whimpers.

"Who saved me?" Daniel asked. He had begun to

think he was wrong to be annoyed with the man and owed him thanks.

"The captain," Ed said.

Ross was laughing again. "I never seen your equal for accidents, Six and a Half. Neither has Trueheart, I do believe. You worry her a lot."

At the station they got him upstairs, the dog hopping after them. Ed stripped off Daniel's oilskins and woolens, sat him on his bed, and pulled the boot off his good leg.

Ross knelt before him. "Give me your other leg." Grinning, he took a knife from his belt. "Got to cut it off."

"He means your boot," Ed said.

With Trueheart overseeing the operation, Ross slit the boot, pulled it off, and tossed it aside. When Ross peeled his stocking off, Daniel saw that his ankle and foot were huge and already turning purple.

Ross was surprisingly gentle as he examined the injury. "I reckon nothing's broke. What do you say, Ed?"

"Looks like a sprain is all, but a good'un. We better ask the captain if we should send for the doctor."

"You ain't going dancing for a while." Ross looked up at Daniel and lost his grin. "We'll get you something for the pain."

"Bring cold packs and towels," Ed said.

Ross clattered down the stairs. Ed mixed a powder in water and told Daniel to drink it. He raised Daniel's leg on pillows.

"Will I be able to go home with you next leave?"

"Not likely, Dan. I'm sorry. The girls will be disappointed."

Daniel was steeled against complaining about his pain, but the news that he would miss his visit with Rachel and Fannie was more than he could bear without a moan.

FIFTEEN

WHEN DANIEL AWOKE HE FOUND the captain beside him. To Daniel, staring up at him, the captain seemed a great Hercules in a seaman's jacket.

The captain examined Daniel's ankle, asked if he'd been given something for pain, said he thought the doctor was not needed.

"Everybody treating you all right?" the captain asked.

"Yes, sir. I want to thank you for pulling me out and to apologize for spoiling another drill. I'm sorry, sir. I truly am."

The captain smiled. "Daniel, accidents are not a bad thing in a drill. They keep us on our toes, train us to act in an emergency. Think no more about it."

The captain turned away, but Daniel did not want to part with him yet. "Sir, that old man I met on the train, Barnaby something, he said you got a gold medal for heroism. May I see it?"

112

"I don't know where it is, just now."

"You got a medal for heroism and you never told Mother and me and you don't even know where it is?"

"Can't see why they hand those out. We surfmen do no more than our duty."

"Aren't you proud of it?"

"I'd have liked to leave it to my son. If I'd had a son."

"Will you get another medal for saving me?"

The captain laughed, thumped Daniel's good knee, and left.

While Daniel's ankle healed he was not allowed to patrol, attend church, go on leave, or take part in any drills except signal flag. After a while, however, he could hop about the station with a crutch made by Obed.

Daniel even found studying better than boredom. He began to take an interest in his lessons and decided to go beyond what he had to make up, so as to be ahead of his class.

As the days grew shorter and colder, the big stove in the galley became the gathering place for the crew. There, Ross finally teased Daniel into challenging Abner at checkers. Abner beat him soundly, but everyone including Ross rooted so boisterously for Daniel that he quite enjoyed the game.

Now at every beach drill the men improved their time by a few seconds. To Daniel, that seemed to indicate that he was what had slowed the men down, but Obed always said, "Soon as we have you back, Danny, we'll do even better."

As the daily routines dragged on, the smallest events became subjects for merriment, argument, or discussion. Ross reported that a schooner was stranded on the shoals off Pamet, that Pamet surfmen had rowed out and got the vessel afloat and on course, but with no thanks from her captain. Laughing, Ross added, "Sore as a boil at being shamed before his men."

Ed sighted an overturned catboat. Obed and Abner rowed out in a high wind, righted the boat, and pulled two boys from the sea. Ross said somebody should blister their hides for taking their boat out in such weather, but Obed said they'd been punished enough.

After a while, even what the men found on the beach made a welcome diversion. Abner brought back a quarter-board, warped and bleached, but with the vessel's name still legible, *Abbey W. Pettigrew*. Obed came upon seals, which Jon said were rare in these parts. Will found a seaman's jacket in the surf. In one pocket was a faded letter signed, "All my dearest love, Beth." Will stared at the letter a long time before he put it back and hung the jacket up to dry and await claim.

Such a long stretch followed in which nothing happened at all that Daniel complained of boredom.

Edwin said, "We can't let ourselves be bored. We must never ease up on drills, patrols, or watches, and never ever take weather or sea for granted."

"This is how we have to live," Will added. "Weeks of routine and then sometimes two or three wrecks in one storm."

Ross grinned. "I guess Six and a Half would like rescues spaced nice and even, once a week, maybe."

In November, the captain said Daniel could resume his duties and assigned him to day watch with Abner. To make the steep climb to the watch house, Daniel still had to hold grimly to the manrope and struggle to keep going. Since Abner always went up first, Daniel managed to conceal how hard it was for him to climb.

On watch, Abner was a different man from the one who traded jokes, pranks, and insults with Ross. On watch, Abner did not like to talk or even to answer questions. Daniel spent three tedious days with him. On the following night the coast was hit by a storm. To Daniel the wind and rain seemed furious—roaring, whistling, and battering the windows with blasts of sand. Breakers crashed and boomed, rising higher and higher, threatening the upper beach and even the station.

But Ed said this was not a bad one. Obed and Ross went out with oilskins, boots, and lanterns to patrol to north and south as calmly as though it were a moonlit night in spring.

Ross returned from his Pamet River patrol with nothing to report. Soon afterward Obed came into the mess with a gust of rain, shouting, "Shipwreck off Nauset!"

The surfmen rushed in from all directions.

"No call for us, Captain," Obed said, stripping off his boots. "Nauset and Orleans are there already. The wreck's on the bars between their stations, three hundred yards out."

"All safe off the vessel?" the captain asked.

"No, sir. Three still missing. But they saved nine."

Abner brought biscuits and a steaming mug of coffee for Obed while the men gathered around him at the table.

"Any dead?" the captain asked.

"Yes, sir. One. The captain's wife. She rolled in with the breakers, lashed to a spar."

Gasps went up all around. The men's dismay surprised Daniel. He had expected them to be used to such news.

"And the captain?" Jon asked.

"Missing with two others. One of them his son."

"His son!" More gasps arose and looks of horror were shared. Ed and Jon, whose turn it was to go out next, brought their gear and dressed while they listened. The others stood in silence while Obed spoke, but whenever he paused to sip coffee, they were at him with questions. What vessel? Where from? Where bound? What cargo?

"A bark, the *Jesse Belle* from Rio, bound for Boston, with three thousand bags of coffee. All swept away."

"Should be an ocean of brew by morning." Ross grinned. "We can take our mugs on patrol."

Obed glared. "It ain't right to be funning at this."

Daniel waited up with the others for Jon to return from his patrol toward Nauset. He did not bring much news. The rescued seamen had been taken to Nauset station, but they were so frozen, exhausted, and confused they could hardly talk. They were given dry clothes and hot drinks and put to bed. Later, they would be given free passage to Boston on the Old Colony Railroad. There was no word about those missing.

SIXTEEN

WITH THE STORM RAGING, Daniel had a bad night, sleepless and obsessed by terrifying thoughts. In mind's eye he saw a spar tumbling in the breakers with a woman bound to it head to toe, a weirdly smiling woman, with wide-open blue eyes, red cheeks, long golden hair streaming in the water.

Then he was aware that it was dawn, without wind or rain, and even the sea was hushed. Mist hung low, shrouding everything beyond the surf.

Daniel and Abner were called to the captain. He looked up only briefly.

"You'll have to patrol. Take Nauset. Are Will and Obed back?"

"Yes, sir. Just back," Abner said.

"Ask them to see me, please. I'll have to send one of them out again to Pamet."

"Yes, sir. Come on, Daniel. Let's get into our gear."

118

"Be there in a minute." Daniel shut the captain's door. "Permission to patrol with Will or Obed, sir."

"Can't you do the longer patrol? Your ankle still bad?"

Daniel knew he might use that as an excuse, but to lie was not the way of a gentleman. Nor was it the way of a surfman, as he now knew.

"It's not that, sir. Abner is boring. He never says a word to me except to give me orders."

The captain turned away. "Denied."

"Sir, I don't see what difference—"

"You are not here to be entertained. Every man on this crew has to work with every other man."

Daniel stood fuming. He had thought his feelings for his uncle were changing. But how could they, when the man was so unreasonable?

"Dismissed," the captain said.

On the beach Daniel tramped peevishly at Abner's heels. Mist surrounded them. The breakers were large, heavy, and sluggish. The sand was littered with seaweed, driftwood, shells, dead gulls, and strange fish. Daniel could see so little beyond the surf that he thought the patrol useless.

Abner stopped abruptly. "Something's out there."

A chill ran over Daniel. He followed Abner's gaze, but the rollers looked a uniform gray, with only a fringe of greenish foam where they broke.

"I don't see anything." He felt he had to whisper.

"See the big one coming in, that dark patch tumbling?"

119

"No, sir."

Abner dashed toward the sea.

Daniel ran after him. "Abner! You're not going out? Let's get a boat! A rope, at least!" Daniel had heard of surfmen who plunged into a heavy sea to save someone and were saved from the undertow themselves only by a line about the waist, pulled in by their mates.

But Abner was at the water's edge, stripping off his oilskins, jacket, and boots. He thrust them at Daniel and splashed into the sea. The surf washed up to his armpits. He kept on. Breakers crashed over him. Up to his neck, he struck out, diving through the breakers. In a moment Daniel could see only his flashing arms. Then he saw nothing.

Daniel ran up and down the beach looking for him in anguish. Should he go after him? Good swimmer though he was, Daniel was sure he had no hope of saving Abner, and it would only mean his own death. But he knew that no surfman would fail to act.

He dropped Abner's gear on the sand and splashed into the surf, shouting, "Abner!"

Then he saw Abner holding something in one arm, swimming with the other. A breaker, huge and black as a whale, was following him.

"Look out, Abner!" Daniel screamed above the roar. The sea broke over Abner's head and swallowed him. Daniel saw his body tumbling to shore, rolling over and over, helpless as a log. Daniel went crashing out. Abner's body slammed against Daniel's legs and staggered him, but Daniel grabbed the man's arm and pulled him to his feet. Together they struggled toward shore, the surf tugging at their knees. Abner turned to look out to sea again.

"What happened, Abner?" Daniel cried.

"I lost him in the undertow."

"Was he alive?"

"Just look, dammit! See if you see anything."

Daniel stood with Abner in the surf, staring about. At last Abner splashed back to shore. Water streamed from his clothes and hair. He picked up his clothes from the beach and began walking back toward the station.

Shivering, soaked to the waist, Daniel hurried after him.

"Keep an eye out," Abner said. "He may come ashore again."

Daniel stared at the breakers reluctantly. He did not want to see whatever it was that might come ashore. They walked on until their watch house on the cliff came into view through wisps of fog.

Abruptly Abner dashed ahead. Running after him, Daniel saw something rolling in with the surf. At first it seemed to be the sort of thing Daniel had been stepping over on the beach. Then it appeared to be a bundle of rags.

But before he reached it, Daniel saw that it was a body, the body of a small boy, rocking gently on the edge of the surf. Foam spilled over the face, filled the mouth, and slipped out between gray lips.

Abner scooped the body up, carried it to drier beach, and laid it down. He fell to his knees beside it.

Daniel followed. "Oh, Abner." That was all he could say but he could not stop saying it. "Oh, Abner. Oh."

Daniel had not wanted to see the body, but now he could not take his eyes away. The face was glossy and puffy but looked oddly serene, eyes closed, long soft lashes on the cheeks, light hair pasted to the forehead in strands. Somewhere Daniel had seen a face like this one, bluish gray with puffy cheeks and gently smiling lips. Both faces were beautiful, except that the other one was pocked. Where had he seen the other one? Daniel could not remember.

The boy was wearing a seaman's jacket that nearly covered his short trousers. One leg had a brown woolen stocking and a boot neatly buttoned. The other leg was bare, with a slab of skin hanging from a ghastly white kneecap. The foot was like a doll's, with trim blue toenails. The boy's arms, covered by the long sleeves, were clutching something to his chest.

Abner murmured, "Oh, God, he's the same age."

Abner doubled over and began to cough. Daniel tried to think of what should be done. "Abner, can't we, you know, do resuscitation?"

Abner spoke to the body. "I'm sorry. We're too late. Oh, we can't save you."

Abner struggled to his feet. He looked like a stiff old man as he picked up the body and cradled it tenderly, as though it could still feel pain.

"Daniel, give me your handkerchief," he said. As Abner wiped the boy's face and hair, something dropped to the sand. Daniel picked it up. It was a wooden monkey, with hinged arms and a human grin.

Abner began walking. Daniel ran after him.

"Where are you going?" Abner barked.

"We're taking him to the station, aren't we?"

"I am. You finish the patrol."

Daniel stopped.

"Take the check from my pocket. Go meet the surfman from Nauset. You know how we do. Say we've found the boy from the *Jesse Belle*. Don't stand there, go on! And don't forget to keep a watch to sea. That's why we go, remember."

"Yes, sir." Daniel found the check. He held out the monkey. "Take this, please, Abner. It belongs to him."

"Put it in my pocket. Now, move!"

Cradling the boy's body, Abner started for the station not with his usual free and gangly stride, but oddly listing.

SEVENTEEN

WITH ABNER'S METAL CHECK cold in his wet mitten, Daniel trudged back toward Nauset. Staring seaward, he tried to penetrate the ragged fog, worst enemy of seaman and surfman. "Please, God, don't let us have another wreck."

It seemed hours that he struggled on. His boots became leaden. The pouch of flares dragged at his belt. When at last he saw the halfway house through the mist, he tried to hurry, but he felt as though he were still wading in surf.

The house was like the one toward Pamet River, hardly taller than a man, but a welcome sight, with smoke wisping from its narrow chimney. Daniel tugged the door open.

The surfman from Nauset was sitting on the table, swinging one leg, with his oilskins, cap, scarf, and mittens beside him. He was a slim young man but already bald.

"Fred Marshall." Grinning, he added, "You must be Six and a Half. Patrolling by yourself now, are you? What took you so long? I was thinking I'd have to go look for you."

Daniel felt weak, hardly able to breathe under the weight of his wet clothes.

"Come in. That's what we usually do. Shut the door, why don't you?"

When Daniel failed to move, Fred got up, pulled him inside, and shut the door. He looked at Daniel closely. "You all right?"

"We found . . . we found . . ."

Fred's lean face was not smiling any longer. "Found?"

"A body." Daniel began to tremble. "In the breakers. Abner . . ."

"Abner?" Fred prompted.

"Swam to save him. But lost him. Then we found him washed ashore. It was too late. Oh, he was so little and he had a toy monkey."

Fred was pulling off Daniel's oilskins, cap, and mittens. Abner's check clattered to the floor. Fred scooped it up then helped Daniel off with his jacket.

"How'd you sponge up so much seawater?" Fred asked. "Go out yourself, did you?"

Fred draped the jacket, cap, and mittens near the stove. Daniel's trembling turned to racking shudders that seemed to come from something outside him, something besides cold. He could not control them.

Fred pulled up a chair. "Sit down, Daniel."

125

He held something to Daniel's lips. "Drink."

After a few swallows of hot, strong coffee, Daniel was able to hold the mug for himself. He was surprised to see how fat and red his hands had become.

"We never get used to finding them," Fred said. "It's always a shock."

"He was a child. It shouldn't happen to a child." Daniel thought he was silent for a long time before he said, "I saw my father dead. My grandparents, too. And my Aunt Mercy."

Fred was sitting on the table, looking at him. "That's not the same. You were prepared for that."

Daniel traced the mug handle with his thumb. "This mug is cracked."

"I know."

"Don't put anything hot in this mug. It's cracked."

"It's been cracked a long time." Fred took it from him.

Daniel remembered something. "I'm supposed to say . . ."

Fred nodded. "The boy was off the *Jesse Belle*. His name was Peter Jory Bushman, age five and a half."

"He had on a man's jacket. Some sailor—"

"The mate. He was holding the boy in the rigging. But the rigging crashed into the sea and the boy was swept away."

"The woman tied to the spar, was she his mother?"

"Yes, and a pity, so mangled and lacerated. But she must have been beautiful. We haven't found the captain or the ship's cook, a lad of fifteen. Afraid we have to count them lost. The bodies will likely wash up near Highland or Peaked Hill Bars. Tell your patrol to pass the word."

"Yes, sir."

"We'd better start back. Can you make it?"

Daniel nodded. Fred helped him into his jacket, which was still damp but now warm, and then his oilskins.

"Our checks," Daniel said.

"I have yours. Here's mine." Fred put it in Daniel's pocket.

"Tell your captain that the *Jesse Belle*'s mate will take the train to Boston tomorrow to report. And he'll give the news to the young cook's parents and the captain's mother."

"Oh, I don't like this." Daniel thought his tears would shame him until he saw that Fred's eyes were brimming, too.

"I wouldn't be that mate for all the treasure on the *Whydah*," Fred said.

The fog was thinner as Daniel started back. The breakers were lighter and the surf seemed to be rushing in faster. Daniel kept his eyes to sea, now and then aware of a vessel riding serenely, but he was otherwise so absent in thought that he was surprised when his station's watch house came into view. He went straight to the captain in his sandy boots and oilskins.

The captain listened to Daniel's report and made notes slowly, as though he found them hard to write.

Daniel asked, "Where is the boy, sir?"

"Obed has laid him out in the infirmary."

"May I go up?"

"Sure you want to?"

Daniel stopped only to change his clothes. He could now hardly believe what he had experienced.

But the dead boy was there, washed and combed, with a sheet draped over his legs. He was dressed in a big white shirt that looked new, no doubt the one Obed's grandmother had just made for him. The sleeves were turned back and the boy's hands were laid on his chest, holding the grinning monkey.

At supper, the captain prayed for the lost and the survivors. The men ate in silence. They often glanced at Daniel and kept offering him food, but he had no appetite.

Daniel went up to his table and wrote to his mother as cheerfully as he could, avoiding any reference to his sadness. To Arthur he gave a full account, adding, "When old or sick people die it's sad and you miss them, but it doesn't seem wrong. But the death of a child seems cruel and unfair. It made me angry, made me want to rage at somebody, but who is there to rage against? Seeing that child made me realize that death can come at any time, even to you and me, Arthur. It grows closer with every breath we take.

"Now I see how precious our days are, even our minutes. Once spent, they will never come again. Arthur, you have always passed your time well, enjoying the present while you work for the future. How did you grow so wise so young?

"About Abner. I've told you how greedy and crude he is. Well, today I saw something in him that I never suspected. I don't mean his courage; I never doubted that. What I saw was his heart, full of love and pity.

"The men here have deep feelings. They joke, tease, play checkers and tiddlywinks, but they are caring and full of purpose. Much more than I have been. You will be surprised to hear this, Arthur, but I used to be rather shallow."

The men were subdued while the boy's body lay in the infirmary, but a frenzy of housekeeping ensued when a letter arrived from the dead boy's grandmother saying that she and her nephew would come for him and go on to Nauset for the body of her daughter-in-law.

The day she was expected, Edwin, Obed, and Daniel waited in the mess while Will kept a lookout at the door. When Wilbur's cart appeared, the captain and the men all went out to watch Charity step carefully down the sand to the station. In the cart behind Wilbur was a little woman in black.

The captain hurried to take her bag and help her get out. Daniel expected a wrinkled, white-haired woman, but Mrs. Bushman looked young, with the same round cheeks and shapely mouth as her grandson. She clung to the captain's arm as she walked unsteadily over the sand.

"Captain, your letter telling me Peter was found was very kind, such a comfort so soon after I heard the news."

"We are all so sorry for your loss, Mrs. Bushman."

The captain opened the door for her and the men trooped in after them. As the captain introduced them, she had a handshake and a smile for each. Her hands were small and plump, like those of her grandson.

She spoke calmly. "My nephew is arranging for the coffins. He'll be along in the morning."

"Me and Charity will bring him, Captain," Wilbur said.

"You must be tired, Mrs. Bushman," Edwin said. "Wouldn't you like to rest a bit before—"

"And have some tea," Obed said. "I've made nut muffins."

"Thank you both. Later, if you don't mind. I'd like to see Peter first." She turned to the captain. "May I?"

"Take Mrs. Bushman's things to my office, Daniel," the captain said.

Holding her bag and wraps, Daniel stood with the men at the foot of the stairs while the captain led her up. Her quiet words floated down to them. "My son took his wife and child on every voyage. They never wanted to be separated. I am so thankful they are not separated now."

The captain came down alone.

"How is she, Captain?" Will asked.

"She will bear up."

Edwin said, "It's soon over for those who die at sea, but the ones they leave behind must suffer on and on."

"Usually the women."

When Mrs. Bushman came down, her only sign of distress was a handkerchief balled in her fist.

130

"You've done well by Peter," she said.

"It was Obed laid him out," Will said.

"Did you find him, Obed?"

"No, it was Daniel, here."

Daniel said, "It was Abner. But I was with him on patrol."

"I'd like to speak to Abner."

"I'm sorry; this is his day off," the captain said.

She turned to Daniel. "Can you tell me . . . ?"

"He was in the surf, not far from here."

Mrs. Bushman was waiting to hear more, but Daniel did not know what else to say.

"How did he look?" she asked. "Frightened? Or in pain, do you think?"

"No, peaceful, like the statue of a baby angel I've seen near my father's grave."

The men stared at him. Mrs. Bushman touched her crumpled handkerchief to her eyes. Daniel was afraid he had blundered. But she smiled. She kissed him.

"Thank you, Daniel. I shall always treasure what you said."

EIGHTEEN

THE CAPTAIN OFFERED MRS. BUSHMAN his room for the night, but she did not want to leave her grandson alone. Obed made up a bed for her in the infirmary.

The next morning Wilbur came with Mrs. Bushman's nephew, a young man with the same delicate family features. They took the boy's body away in a little casket of polished wood.

Daniel felt mournful all day. That night he dreamed about a casket filled with wildflowers, tossing on the breakers. He awoke feeling nauseated and could not eat. He felt even worse when Ed came back from patrol with news that the body of Captain Bushman had washed ashore at Peaked Hill Bars, just east of Provincetown. It was thought the body of the young cook would never be found.

"It's a terrible coast, Danny," Obed said. "It ain't called

Ocean Graveyard for nothing. Many a vessel's been lost and many a body swallowed up."

The captain called Daniel to his office.

He said, "I've been meaning to tell you that you've done well lately. You're becoming one of us."

Daniel thought so, too, up to a point. He was now as good as anybody with signal flags and resuscitation. He had even been rowing with the men without disgracing himself. But since the injury to his ankle, he had been left out of the beach-apparatus drill. He was afraid he would not be allowed to take part in the contest with Pamet River.

While Daniel had grown to admire the surfmen and even to like some of them warmly, he was confused by his feelings for his uncle. Often he was in awe of him and sometimes longed to be closer to him when he saw the likeness to his grandfather. Yet when his uncle was harder than Daniel thought necessary, Daniel remained resentful.

Daniel stood before his uncle now, wanting yet unwilling to respond to what he had just said.

His uncle was looking at him thoughtfully. "Daniel, I know you've experienced some harsh realities lately."

Thinking that he would have been spared those realities if the captain had not ordered him to patrol with Abner, Daniel stood mute.

"Sometimes it helps to talk things over."

"No, thank you. Sir!"

"As you wish, then, Daniel. Dismissed."

On Sunday when the duty roster changed, Daniel was surprised to see that he was assigned to the north patrol, sunset till eight P.M., with Jon.

Daniel had seen less of Jon than of the other men. When not on duty, Jon was usually in his room next to the infirmary with paperwork of his own to do. In the mess, he often sat apart with a book, his dog on her mat near his chair.

Daniel struggled against being intimidated by Jon's formal manner and great physique. He felt more at ease with the other men, even those he did not like. Daniel did not see Jon as a gentleman and yet Jon had a gentleman's qualities. He was poised, well spoken, well educated, and his manners surpassed Daniel's own.

The captain had said that every man must work well with every other man. Now Daniel was sure the captain was sending him out with Number One because he had overheard Daniel talking to Will one day.

"Jon gets on my nerves," Daniel had told Will. "He has no feelings, no more than an old wooden Indian."

"Oh, Jon has feelings," Will had said. "It's just not his nature to show them. And he's not old, he's only three years older than I am."

"Well, I don't understand him. What goes on in that bony head of his?"

"If you can get him to talk some time, you might be surprised."

When Daniel set out with Jon, twilight was still on the sands, but deepening quickly. Jon walked on the edge of the surf with his great dog at heel, although she fell back or ran ahead now and then to sniff here and there, to splash through the foam, or to make her own alert scrutiny of the breakers.

Tramping along in Jon's wake, Daniel was angry with his uncle for putting him with this strange man. He thought of what Obed had told him, that Jon's family had been Christians for generations, belonging to what were called the Praying Indians who lived in their own village, Mashpee. But not in that or in anything else he knew about Jon could Daniel find any common ground with him.

Annoyed at being in awe of the man, Daniel felt a need to assert himself. "Did the captain tell you what I said about you?"

Jon was scanning the horizon. "No, Daniel."

"Want to know what I said?"

"If it would please you to tell me."

"I said you're like something carved out of a tree that learned to walk and talk but not to feel."

Daniel studied Jon's profile in the fading light, looking for a reaction. If he had not been sure the man had no sense of humor, he might have thought he saw the flicker of a smile.

"You walk all right but you certainly don't talk much. Think you're too good for the rest of us?"

"No. Different in some ways, the same in others. As it is with everybody."

"Ross says you claim King Philip was your ancestor."

"King Philip is what the English called him. His name was Metacomet. He was not my ancestor."

Daniel laughed. "So why is Ross telling that lie?"

"He wasn't lying, just mistaken. He meant Massasoit, Metacomet's father."

"The great sachem? Claimed to rule the whole peninsula?"

"He did that and much beyond."

"Then why don't you straighten Ross out?"

"It doesn't matter."

"Then straighten me out."

"I am descended from another child of Massasoit, a daughter named Amie."

"How do you know?"

"From the genealogy compiled and published by my mother's cousin Zerviah Gould Mitchell."

Daniel was impressed. He did not like the feeling. "So what," he muttered.

The dog ran up to look into Daniel's face, investigating. He gave her a rub and she went back to her own affairs.

Jon had that twitch of a smile again, but his eyes calmly swept the ocean. Daniel was irked by Jon's lack of response.

"I think it's hooey that you went to Harvard. Isn't it? Tell me the truth."

Jon stopped and looked at him with great, dark, burning eyes. Shocked, Daniel saw the face of a warrior in ambush.

But Jon's tone was that of a civilized man. "I speak the truth or I hold my tongue."

When Jon walked on, Daniel followed. The warrior had only stared; he had not killed him. Daniel forced himself to rally. "Then tell me. Did you really go to Harvard?"

"Yes. The college was meant for Indians as well as English from the very beginning."

"What did you want to go for, anyway?"

"I thought to become a lawyer for my people."

"Then why didn't you? Too much book learning for you?"

Daniel knew this could not be true, because more than any of the surfmen, even more than the captain, Jon was a reader.

"I can't live within walls." Jon answered as though to a friendly question. "I like the sky, the wind, the seasons. I like to look out over the sea to the rim of the earth."

"What about working for your people?"

"I came to know that all people are my people."

Having riled the Indian once without much result, Daniel grew bolder. "I wonder about that. Are you really human? You never show any human faults."

"Oh, I have faults."

"What faults? You drink firewater in secret?"

Again came the twitch of a smile. "No."

"What, then?"

Daniel thought Jon ought to say it was none of his business, but Jon answered, "Pride."

Daniel would have agreed that Jon was haughty, but

he did not see that as pride, nor did he see pride as a fault. Daniel liked himself best when he was proud of himself.

"What's wrong with pride? I wouldn't give a rap for a man without pride."

"Our Lord has said the meek shall inherit the earth."

Although Daniel recognized the courtesy and gravity of Jon's reply, something stubborn in him would not soften.

"What do you think it's wrong to be proud of, then? Your strength, your brain, your ancestry?"

"Yes. And all this." Jon's long arm swept ocean, sky, and earth.

"You mean you still claim all this?"

"Yes. It is mine and not mine. Yours and not yours. It belongs to everyone but not to anyone."

"That doesn't make sense."

"The earth belongs to God, the Great Spirit, and to us also, because we are part of it. That makes me proud."

"I don't see—"

"Is the pine tree proud? The gull? The doe? Is Trueheart proud? They live in all simplicity and will inherit the earth, but shall I? I should be meek, as they are, but I take pride in what God has made me, a human being. Of all living things, only a human being can see the beauty of earth and the mysterious power that God gave her to make life and take it away."

"If you think God gave earth the right to take life, why are you a surfman, saving people?"

"I act in the strength God gave me. If I save a life, I

138

have done it through his will. His will also if I fail. Still I am proud to be God's instrument. But pride is wrong."

"So that's why you don't care what happens." Daniel wondered if Jon would admit his lack of feeling.

"If God has me succeed, I am happy that sorrow was prevented. If not, I am sad but I accept God's decision. So must we all, Daniel."

Daniel fell behind again. No doubt the captain had heard Will suggest that he get Jon to talk. Perhaps it was for that reason the captain had sent him out with Jon, as much as to have them work together.

NINETEEN

DANIEL WROTE TO ARTHUR, "You'll be surprised to hear this, but I can't do the job of Number Six as well as Will does it, not in time for the beach-apparatus contest, anyway. I haven't been allowed to take part since I sprained my ankle. So I must do what's best for the crew and play victim. Every day I mean to go out and climb a bit higher on the wreck pole until I can make it to the top. I shall do it or be killed trying.

"Of course, I don't expect to be killed. I remember what you said when I was learning to ride my cycle. My body can do it, it's only my mind that holds me back."

To himself, Daniel added that if Obed could throw up every day and still go to school, he, Daniel, could conquer heights.

Early the next morning, Daniel slipped out through the mess, avoiding the galley where he could hear Will, whose turn it was to cook, already clattering about.

Quiet surf was swishing up and back on the beach. The breakers were low and gray. It was dark overhead, but a red haze shimmered on the horizon where the sun would soon appear. Brushing through the patches of dewy grass between the station and the wreck pole, he got his trousers damp to the knee. He was chilled through, as much from nerves as from the weather.

Daniel had no idea how he had reached the top of the pole the first time. He recalled climbing spike after spike as in a nightmare, yielding to the urge to look down, then beach, surf, and breakers spinning around his head until he blacked out.

Somehow he had reached the crow's-nest. It seemed that some force outside of him had kept him going. But he had not gained strength from that climb. Rather, his fear was greater, and the force, whatever it was, had left him.

"I am not afraid today," he told himself. "Today I am only climbing two spikes."

But the first spike was higher than he remembered. When he placed his slippery boot on it and took hold overhead, his hands broke out in sweat.

He forced himself to stay on the spike, paused for breath, pulled his body up, and paused again. To keep from looking down or closing his eyes, he stared out to sea. The firm horizon seemed to steady him and everything else as well. The sea did not tilt. The sky did not spin. He felt a surge of hope and joy.

On the next day, however, the ocean was layered with moving fog and the wind was gusting. Clouds

141

obscured the horizon. The rising sun was a pink, wobbly gel. Going up, Daniel had to stop and cling to the pole until his dizziness subsided.

Walking back to the station, he thought of wearing his suede gloves to give his sweaty hands the grip he needed.

He found Will watching from the doorway of the galley.

"You don't have to do this, you know," Will said.

"I want to," Daniel said. "I mean to be in the contest. I don't want any pity."

"I don't pity you. I was being realistic."

"Which means you don't believe I can do it."

"Actually, I believe you can. Let me help."

Will began going out to stand at the foot of the pole while Daniel climbed, encouraging him as Arthur had done with the bicycle. "Keep going! You can do it!"

After a week of secret work, adding a few rungs up at a time, Daniel could scramble swiftly to the top.

He was elated, but he said to Will, "Know what's hardest for me? Stepping off the crow's-nest into the breeches buoy."

The next morning just at daybreak, Will woke him. "Come down to the boat room."

There Daniel found the breeches buoy strung up from a beam in the ceiling with a ladder beside it.

"For you to practice getting in and out when no one's around," Will said. "The captain gave us permission."

Will taught him how to grasp the ropes, wrap them securely around his wrists, swing out, ease his legs into the breeches, and slip into the buoy. Daniel worked every day and practiced his knots as well. On the eve of the last drill before the contest, Will said, "Nobody could do better!"

The next morning, Daniel knocked on the captain's door.

"May I be victim in the drill today, sir?"

"Good morning, Daniel." The captain smiled.

"Good morning, sir. I want to be victim in the contest, too. If I may, sir."

"Permission granted."

Will was waiting for him. "What did the captain say?"

"Permission granted. No questions."

"Of course not. He trusts you can do it if you say so."

After breakfast, with the men assembled in the boat room, the captain announced the change in assignment. No one protested, but Ross whispered, "Why the Sunday gloves? Afraid to blister your dainty hands?"

The men rushed the cart out and down to the beach, Trueheart with them. Daniel ran to the wreck pole. When the captain called, "Action!" Daniel scrambled up, hands firm in his gloves, feet steady on the spikes, and quickly reached the crow's-nest. He pulled off his gloves and when the shot line came, snatched it, made it fast, and signaled to the captain. Out came the hawser. Daniel tied it above the tail block. The breeches buoy came lurching toward him. He pulled it close, grasped the ropes, and swung into the breeches. The buoy went squealing down on its tackle. The captain and Number One helped him get out.

"Three minutes, forty-five seconds," the captain said.

"That'll do 'er!" Abner cried. "We'll best Pamet River and no mistake!"

Will, Obed, and Ed surrounded Daniel and pounded him on the back. Daniel had never felt happier.

TWENTY

THE DAY OF THE CONTEST BROKE clear and pleasant, the sea brilliant, the surf foaming and sparkling. To Daniel, even the gulls seemed excited, wheeling above the station.

At breakfast the men joked, teased, and gobbled down even more hotcakes than usual, but Daniel could not eat.

"Do we go to Pamet River for the contest?" he asked.

Ross laughed. "Ain't that just like Six and a Half? How does he think we can man our posts, if we go traipsing off?"

Will said, "The Pamet River crew will drill at their own station, with both captains and the district superintendent keeping time. Then those who can will come here for our drill."

Villagers began arriving early, on foot and in carts and buggies. So many horses were soon tethered near

145

the sheds and outhouses that latecomers had to leave their carts and horses up by the roadside, among the scrub pines.

Wilbur brought his wife and Obed's grandmother, along with the news that a crowd had already gathered at Pamet River, that Abner's wife could not come because their son was feverish, and that Ross's wife would not come because she'd had enough of beach drills.

Visitors swarmed over the station. Children scampered about, squealing and shouting. Trueheart was ecstatic. Ed took the children on a tour of the boat room, and Obed handed out molasses cookies.

Daniel watched for Rachel and Fannie. When at last he saw them walking down the slope toward the station, he rushed to meet them.

"I was afraid you weren't coming!" he cried.

"We'd have been here sooner, but Aunt Violet was feeling poorly," Rachel said.

Fannie added, "As usual."

"Couldn't she have come, too?" Daniel asked.

"She never goes near the sea," Fannie said. "She claims it bears malice against our family."

"Meaning what?" Daniel asked.

"Meaning she's a ridiculous old woman."

"She has her reasons, Fannie," Rachel said. "Maybe you'll understand some day."

"Where is Will?" Fannie asked.

"On watch. He'll be down for the drill."

A shout went up from the beach. "The captains are coming!"

Surfmen and visitors rushed to the shore. A crowd of hazy figures appeared in the distance. On the shimmering beach, magnified by sun and spray, the people looked huge and appeared to be trudging heartily without advancing. Children ran to meet them, splashing through the surf, heedless of their boots.

"That man beside our captain is district superintendent," Obed told Daniel. "He's more'n sixty but he can still pull a mighty oar. The man with them is captain of Pamet River."

"What was your time, Pamet River?" Ross called when the captains drew near.

The superintendent grinned. "They have a new record."

The Pamet River captain said, "Three minutes, fifty-nine seconds."

Someone cried. "Might as well give over, Perkins Hollow!"

"That's a challenge and no mistake," Ross said, with a wink at Abner.

As the crowd moved along toward Perkins Hollow, Daniel whispered to the girls, "We've done it in three minutes, forty-five seconds."

At Perkins Hollow, the superintendent asked the visitors to stand back against the dunes. Daniel and the crew went off to the boat room, where Will was already waiting. When the men dashed out with the cart, Trueheart running beside them, cheers went up from the crowd. Daniel's nervousness was gone and he felt only sharp elation as he rushed to the wreck pole.

The crew stopped on the beach and stood ready for the signal to begin. The crowd went silent. Only breakers, surf, and squealing gulls could be heard as the two captains and the superintendent consulted their watches.

"Action!" Daniel's uncle shouted.

Daniel climbed the first spike and the next. The spikes were cold, his hands slippery with the sweat of excitement. He had forgotten his gloves. He went stiff with panic. Icy wind on his neck somehow revived him. He clenched his teeth and climbed on with agonizing slowness.

The cannon boomed. Daniel looked up and to his horror saw the line fly overhead and settle across the crow's-nest. He should have been there to retrieve it. He climbed desperately, struggling to make his arms and legs work faster. Minutes seemed to pass before he reached the top. He snatched the line and hitched it to the pole with great care, lest his trembling fingers make a mistake.

He finished with such relief that he forgot for a moment that the captain was waiting for his signal.

Daniel felt time drag as the breeches buoy came lurching toward him. He grasped the ropes supporting the buoy. His hands slipped. He hesitated, afraid to trust his weight to his moist grip. He heard a distant shout.

"Do it, Daniel! You can do it!" Was that Will calling? Or Arthur? Or only in his head?

He took a turn of rope around each wrist and stepped out. His body slumped into the breeches buoy. He flew down, wind in his face. His boots dragged in the sand. The captain hauled him out. He was startled by a roar of cheers.

"Three minutes, fifty-nine seconds," the superintendent said. "Elisha?"

"I make it the same," Daniel's uncle said. The other captain nodded.

Abner shouted, "Well, I'll be jiggered!"

The superintendent turned to the crowd. "We have a tie, folks. The same time exactly."

There was a burst of applause. People rushed up and crowded around the crew, laughing and exclaiming.

"Stand back, please, folks," the superintendent cried. "Let the men stow their gear."

Ross whispered to Daniel, "We should have won, you know."

Daniel felt too guilty and sad to respond. Remembering that he had to climb the wreck pole and undo his knots, he started back along the beach.

Will came after him. "Let me do it, Daniel."

"It's my job!" Burning with failure, Daniel stomped to the pole and climbed up, undid the hitches, let the ropes slip to the beach. He stepped off the crow's-nest onto the spikes. The beach did not tempt him to look down.

He found Will watching him. "You did that without giving it a thought, no more afraid than any other surfman."

Daniel was astonished. "So I did!"

Will laughed. "You've won your battle!"

As they walked back to help put away the gear, Daniel said, "But I made us lose the contest. I'm very sorry."

"We didn't lose! Nobody lost. We all won! Didn't you hear what we decided? Pamet River will provide the food and Obed will cook. Ross is claiming we tied on purpose, so we wouldn't have to eat Pamet River cooking."

As Daniel and Will were coming out of the boat room after everything was stowed away, Fannie rushed up to them, with Rachel following.

"I've never seen the drill done faster!" Fannie cried. "You surfmen are wonderful."

"Congratulations," Rachel said.

"I thought the drill took forever," Daniel said. It was odd what tricks the mind could play. He realized now that his part had actually taken only a few seconds longer.

"Fannie, have you said good-bye to Father?" Rachel asked.

"You're not leaving already!" Will cried.

"We should stay for refreshments at least!" Fannie said.

Rachel turned away. "Fannie, you know our obligations."

They all went up the slope toward the road.

Will said, "Rachel, you're coming early on Thanksgiving, aren't you, to help decorate the boat room?"

Rachel shook her head. "Afraid not, Will."

"But you girls did such a good job last year. Our old boat room never looked so jolly. Anyway, we'll have a grand time, no matter when you get here. Wilbur's bringing his banjo and Barnaby Duff his fiddle, same as before. Daniel, wait till you hear old Barnaby Duff! He can play so fast you'd think his bow would catch fire."

Daniel laughed. Rachel looked away. Fannie scowled.

"We're not coming," Fannie said.

Will stopped short. "Not coming? Not coming at all?"

"We're having dinner with the Yateses," Fannie said. "Father, too. Even Aunt Violet. Mrs. Yates asked us special, because Percy will be home. I don't like it one bit!"

"Thanks for walking up with us," Rachel said. "Please don't trouble to come any farther."

She started off along the road, leaving Fannie to say good-bye and catch up.

TWENTY-ONE

THE DAYS BEFORE THANKSGIVING were the busiest Daniel had seen at the station. Every afternoon, food arrived from the Pamet River surfmen, who more than fulfilled their agreement, sending turkeys, hams, pumpkins, apples, nuts, and jugs of sweet cider. Obed and Will were kept busy cooking and baking. Between drills, patrols, and watches, which nothing was allowed to interrupt, the men scoured, shined, and polished the station top to bottom.

On Thanksgiving morning, planks and trestles were brought in from the sheds to make extra tables in the mess and benches around the walls. The cart and boats were moved outdoors.

Young people from Fleetport brought leaves, stalks, and pumpkins to decorate the boat room. The surfmen's families came early. Abner's small, quiet wife brought her small, quiet son and kept him close at her side. Ross's wife, Adah, was taller than he and plump, jolly, and bossy. She ordered her two rowdy boys to help in the mess and galley.

Jon's sister, Leah, and her four children arrived on foot. Daniel saw them come swinging down the slope from the road, Leah with a large basket on her hip, the children running ahead. The youngest, a girl, scrambled up the cliff to the watch house, shouting, "Uncle Jon! Uncle Jon!"

Like her brother, Leah was tall with glossy black hair and bright oval eyes, but she had none of Jon's stoic manner.

She gave Daniel an impish smile. "You must be Six and a Half."

Daniel laughed. "I didn't think Jon noticed that."

"Maybe he hasn't. A Nauset surfman from our village told me. How do you like working with that brother of mine?"

"Well." Daniel paused. "He's a splendid surfman."

"But you find it hard to understand him." She laughed. "So do I. At home he mostly sits in a corner and reads. I think my little one knows him best. Anyway, she says she is going to be a Number One surfman, just like him."

She and Fannie both, Daniel thought, but by now Fannie knew it was not going to happen. It was too bad, in a way, for girls with such spirit.

"I have corn cakes for the party," Leah said. "But I'm sure you don't need them."

Villagers from Fleetport and Truro brought so many

cakes, breads, cookies, pies, tarts, candies, cheeses, and jars of preserves that Daniel was afraid the tables would not hold Obed's turkeys, hams, and chowder.

After the captain's prayer of thanksgiving, guests and surfmen lined up while Obed, Will, and Daniel carved meat, served vegetables, poured cider. There was so much laughter and confusion that orders were often mixed up, but no one complained. Food stayed on the tables all day for refills and for the surfmen from Pamet River, who came in shifts.

When Wilbur's banjo and Barnaby's fiddle started up, the boat room soon throbbed with stomping and clapping.

The children were rollicking dancers, and so were Ross and Adah. The captain gave Obed's grandmother and all the older ladies a whirl. Jon danced sedately with Leah but she soon left him for livelier partners.

Abner and his wife sat on the sidelines, holding hands, looking on and smiling, while their son slept on Abner's lap. Will, not looking on, not smiling, hung about in corners. The only other one who did not dance was Obed in the galley.

To Daniel's delight, the girls from Fleetport took him for a regular member of the crew. One dark-eyed girl named Prudence seemed to favor him especially. Daniel was pleased with himself until, sipping lemonade between dances, he noticed that her eyes often strayed.

"What's the matter with your friend?" she asked.

"Which friend?"

"Will Ryder, the one who helped you serve. He didn't eat any dinner. He's just been hanging around like a wallflower. Why isn't he dancing?"

"Maybe he doesn't dance."

"Oh, he's a good dancer. He isn't ill, is he?"

Annoyed to see that the interest she had shown him was really for his friend, Daniel was tempted to say Will was spoken for. But that wasn't quite true. Daniel consoled himself with the thought that Prudence was Will's age and it would be good for Will to think of someone other than Rachel.

Daniel said, "Maybe you'd like to dance with him."

"Maybe. But I have to say hello to my cousins."

She went off to join two girls near the window, but Daniel saw that her eyes followed him to Will.

Will was lounging in the doorway, staring at the floor, thumbs looped in his pockets.

"Why aren't you doing your duty by the girls?"

Will sighed. "It's a bad sign, you know."

"What's a bad sign?"

"Rachel and her whole family going to Percy's today."

"No, it isn't. It isn't any kind of sign."

"I'm sure it means an arrangement. Rachel may be setting the date this very minute."

"That's ridiculous! Anyway, it won't do any good to worry about it. Why don't you ask Prudence to dance? I happen to think she won't turn you down."

"I want Rachel to be happy. More than anything in this world. If Percy is the one she wants, I won't sulk."

"But you are sulking."

"I can't stand not knowing what I've done to offend her."

"Come on, Will. Barnaby and Wilbur have finished their cider and are tuning up again. Prudence is looking your way."

"I don't know what to do about it, that's the worst," Will said. "I've tried to ask her what's wrong, but she says nothing's wrong. If I insist, she gets annoyed."

"I think Prudence is the prettiest girl here. She's got huge, shiny black eyes, like jet. Ever notice?"

"Fannie said she wasn't allowed to tell me, but she thinks Rachel feels the same as ever about me."

"Then why are you so worried?"

"I don't know what that means. I'm afraid Rachel's feelings never were what I thought." Will was growing more agitated. "I've tried to talk to Ed, but he just says it's Rachel's affair. Ed's not against me, is he?"

"Will, you sound like a crazy man."

"Once Ed told me that appearances can be deceiving. What do you think he meant by that?"

"Listen, Will; they're starting another reel. Put a smile on your face. Ask Prudence to dance. Have some fun. It will be good for you."

Will turned away. "I feel cold. Think I'll go sit by the stove with Obed."

TWENTY-TWO

AFTER THANKSGIVING, ROUTINES at the station went on as usual, but without the usual banter among the surfmen.

"What's the matter with everybody?" Daniel asked Obed.

"It's always like this after the holiday. The men miss their families worse than ever. They start to wonder why they keep this job."

Only the weather was lively, changing almost daily from oddly warm to bitterly cold. Often mist veiled the late autumn sunshine, but vessels passed serenely on course, day and night. The Highland Light swung through wisps of fog, and foghorns blared.

Will rarely spoke. He was sluggish and absent-minded in drills. Patrols took him half an hour longer than usual.

Daniel cornered him. "You said a surfman must always keep his mind on his work."

"I can't help it, Daniel. I told the captain I'd quit, but he said I mustn't leave him short-handed with the worst of the season still ahead. But I'm afraid of making some terrible mistake."

With Christmas approaching, some of the men took to whittling. Abner worked on a ship model for his son. Jon carved beads for his sister's children. Ross made fishing poles for his two boys.

Daniel wrote to his mother that he was not sure what he could get for her and Mrs. O'Till, out here beyond civilization, but for himself he suggested new shirts, gloves, and ties for church.

"Will we have a party?" Daniel asked Obed.

"Thanksgiving is the only party we're allowed."

"What about presents?"

"Most times only children get presents."

A few days before Christmas, Obed came from town bringing the mail and two packages for Daniel.

"What you got there, Six and a Half?" Ross asked. "Something from Santy?"

"Shouldn't think you'd be interested in presents from Santy," Daniel said, starting for the stairs.

"Sure we would, Danny," Obed said, wistfully.

Daniel opened his packages at the table. The larger one was from his mother and Mrs. O'Till and held the expected shirts, ties, and gloves, with books and a note.

Daniel read the note aloud. "The books are for you to share with your friends. It may interest them to know that Walt Whitman, who wrote the poems, is a friend of William O'Connor, second in command of the Life-

158

Saving Service. The stories by Poe may give even the bravest surfmen shivers."

Ross laughed. "The only thing I read that gives me shivers is politics."

The other present was a knife from Arthur.

"Let's see it," Ross said. Daniel gave it to him reluctantly, wary of jibes, but Ross pulled the knife from its sheath and examined it seriously, tested the blade, studied the handle, weighed the balance.

"Give you mine for it," he said with a grin. "Keep it on your belt, Daniel. It's sure to come in handy."

In his thanks to Arthur, Daniel wrote that his knife got the only decent remark Ross had ever made to him.

On Christmas morning, the captain announced that he, Ed, and Will would man the station and everyone else could go to church. Daniel caught Will as he was starting for the watch house. "I'll take your place if you want to go, Will."

"Percy will be there. He would ruin Christmas for me."

"Anything I can say to Rachel for you?"

Will turned away. "Say I wish her a happy Christmas and a happy life."

Daniel put on a new tie and shirt with slickers and boots and set out ahead of the others, planning to see Rachel and hoping still to do something in Will's behalf. It was cold and drizzling, but the walk to the village now seemed easy after his months on patrol. Fannie answered his knock.

"I've come to wish you happy Christmas," Daniel said.

"Come in, come in! Rachel, it's Dan!"

Rachel appeared and gave Daniel her hand and her slow smile. She was pale and seemed thinner than when he had seen her last, but her eyes were still brilliant and her red-gold hair had never looked more beautiful.

"Have you come to escort us to church?" Rachel asked.

"Unless you have other plans," Daniel said.

"Percy said he'd meet us there." Fannie scowled. "He's not even gentleman enough to come get us."

"We're waiting for Aunt Violet," Rachel said. "Come sit a moment, Daniel."

Daniel left his slickers and boots near the door and followed the girls to the parlor. "Too bad you couldn't come for Thanksgiving," Daniel said. "We had a jolly time, but everybody missed you. Especially Will and I."

"I wish we'd been there instead of at Percy's," Fannie said. "What a bore he is, and his mother, too. Can't you see that, Rachel? When he isn't bragging about himself, she's bragging for him. No wonder he's still the spoiled, snooty brat he was in school."

"You didn't know him in school," Rachel said.

"But I've heard all about him. He used to cheat."

"Nobody likes him much," Daniel said. "I heard Prudence and her cousins talking about him at the dance. But everybody likes Will. Especially Prudence."

Fannie said, "That Prudence! She knows a good man when she sees one. Will better watch out."

Rachel got up abruptly and went to the window. "It's

160

clearing up. I'm so glad." She did not sound glad. "Rain at Christmas is so depressing."

"Remember last Christmas, Rachel, how happy we all were?" Fannie said. "You and Will sang a duet in church, like a pair of angels. You looked like you belonged together forever."

Daniel said, "Will isn't happy this Christmas. He can't keep his mind on his work."

Rachel was looking through the parted curtains. She spoke softly. "He'll soon remember how important his work is to him." She leaned her forehead against the windowpane for a moment. When she turned back, she kept her face averted. "I'd better see if Aunt Violet needs help."

After Rachel left the room, Daniel whispered, "Fannie, have you found out what happened between them?"

"No. Rachel doesn't talk to me much these days. But she's always talking to Aunt Violet. Or rather, she mostly listens."

"Have you asked your aunt?"

"No point in that. Aunt Violet doesn't talk to me, either. She knows I have no patience with her nonsense. Anyway, she's addled half the time. But Rachel claims she makes good sense when she's a mind to."

"What does Aunt Violet think of Will?"

"She doesn't like him, although she doesn't even remember his name. She remembers Percy, though. He sees to that, the sneak. He wants her on his side."

Rachel returned with her aunt, who was dressed in

somber purple. Remembering that Aunt Violet was younger than Ed, Daniel was shocked at how thin and stooped she was, with sunken eyes and crumpled cheeks. Although her hair was as dark as Fannie's, it looked brittle.

She stopped abruptly in the doorway and stared at Daniel. "Charlie?" Her voice quavered. "Oh, is it my Charlie? Home at last!" Aunt Violet started toward Daniel, hands outstretched, face transformed by smiles. Before she reached him, she faltered. "Isn't it Charlie?"

"Aunt Violet, this is our friend Daniel Stafford, come to take us to church this morning," Rachel said.

Aunt Violet sat down, pulled out a black handkerchief, and fluttered it before her neck. "Rachel, it's hot in here. You've built up the fire too much."

"No, Auntie, you're warm because you're wearing your shawl. We're going to church. Come, dear, or we'll be late."

"I don't feel like church today."

"Yes, you do," Fannie said. "It's Christmas."

Aunt Violet held out a trembling hand to Daniel. "Will you help me to my feet?" Her fingers were like a bundle of twigs on Daniel's arm.

Daniel had looked forward to walking with the girls, but he had to follow them slowly with their aunt. She mumbled but did not seem to be addressing him.

She looked up suddenly. "You're not one of them, are you? I don't want any of them coming here to court my girls."

"I'm not old enough yet to be courting, Miss Beckers."

She searched his face, then gave him a nod. "Not for a few years, any rate. That other one, he won't be in church today, will he? The one that makes her cry?"

"Do you mean Will Ryder?"

"The less she sees of him, the better. If she takes him, she'll have to cry the more one day. I tell her true. He'd give her a life of fear and sorrow and leave her with nothing, no pension for widows and orphans. She'll have to cry for her father one day, and that's already too much. And what will become of me, when all the men are gone? Rachel understands."

"Understands what, Miss Beckers?" Daniel had a moment of hope that he would learn more from her, but she was mumbling again, paying no more attention to him than if he were a cane for her support.

TWENTY-THREE

DANIEL THOUGHT WILL OUGHT to know that Aunt Violet was somehow involved in Rachel's change of heart, but still he believed it would be unfair to Rachel to reveal what she was trying to keep secret. He thought it might help if he could find out what had turned Aunt Violet against surfmen.

Daniel looked for a chance to question Obed again, but they were not scheduled together and when off duty, other surfmen were always nearby.

Now in January, the weather was bad on some days and worse on others, with sharp winds, sleet, or flurries of snow. Daniel was ahead in his schoolwork and knew from the fit of his clothes that he had grown taller and more muscular. He was glad of all that, but work at the station was hard and the periods of leisure were often boring.

The men snatched at whatever they could find for diversion.

At supper one night in February after Edwin had come back from his day off, Ross asked, "What's going on in town?"

"Not much."

"Must be something. Or is everybody in a coma?"

"The fishermen are taking the covers off their boats, starting to scrape and caulk."

"Early for that, ain't it?" Abner said.

"Spring is coming," Obed said. "Now it's a sure thing."

Ross laughed. "Spring is coming, but scraping and caulking don't bring it."

"What else is new?" Abner asked.

"That last gale damaged my mulberry," Ed said.

"You mean the one you brought back from China?" Abner asked.

"For your wife, your last voyage out before she died?" Obed added.

Ed nodded. "That's the one. Afraid it's done for."

"Oh, that's a pity," Obed said.

Will, who now seldom spoke at meals, said, "Rachel must feel bad. She loved her mother's tree."

"Rachel probably has something else to think about." Ross leered at Will. "Ed, ain't you got something more interesting to tell us? Like some forthcoming family event?"

"Pass the bread, Jon," Edwin said.

"Come on, Ed, you know what I mean," Ross said. "Or hasn't a certain young man popped the question?"

Abner said, "Give over, Ross. Let us eat in peace."

"Some of us think some things count more than food."

Daniel cried, "Ross, shut up!"

"But we've all got Rachel's interest at heart, ain't that so? We're like her uncles, you might say. Tell us. Has he popped the question yet?"

Edwin gave Ross a glance over the rim of his cup.

"Why, that scoundrel!" Ross cried. "Courting her like he done. Leading her on. Leading us all on, you might say, making us think we'd be dancing at her wedding."

Edwin spoke into his cup. "He has put the question."

Ross pounded the table, laughing. "What a catch! Son of the richest man in Fleetport."

Will jumped up, scarlet to the ears. His chair crashed to the floor.

"Pay that no heed, Will," Ed said. "She hasn't said yes."

"Has she said no?"

"She hasn't said anything, yet."

Will dashed out of the mess.

On the next Sunday, Ross, Ed, and Will were at church, Abner on watch, and the captain and Jon working on their endless reports. Daniel found Obed alone at last, in the galley mixing pie dough. It was not Daniel's turn to help with meals, but he offered to peel apples.

"Obed, do you know anybody named Charlie?"

"Well, there's Charlie Kent, runs the livery stable. Goes by Charles, though, not Charlie."

"Does he look like me?"

Obed giggled. "More like me, I'd say. For size, that is. But he's bald and past seventy."

"Know any other Charlies?"

"Charlie Ingalls, that was one of us surfmen here."

"Does he favor me, by any chance?"

Obed looked up from his rolling pin. "You might say that. Dark hair like yours. Young-looking for his age."

"Is he a friend of Aunt Violet's?"

Obed was rolling dough again. After a while, he said, "They was all but married. The date was set for June. He was killed in April."

"Oh, I see! Oh, that's terrible. How did it happen?"

"Queer sort of accident. He disappeared during boat drill. We stayed out all night, looking for him. No one ever found him. He never washed ashore anywhere."

"Oh, I understand. That must be why Aunt Violet says the sea bears malice against her family."

"Seems like."

Daniel thought about it as he worked on apples. "But other women get over losing their men to the sea."

Obed said quietly, "For her it was worse than most."

"How?"

"Never mind, Danny. Best to forget. Best if she'd forget, too."

"Don't you want to help Will?"

"How can it help Will if I tell you about Aunt Violet?"

167

"I'm sure she's turned Rachel against marrying a surfman. But I think Rachel won't ask Will to choose between her and the service, because she knows how much the service means to him. She doesn't even want Will to know how she feels."

Obed fitted the dough into a pie plate, twirled the plate on his fingertips, and deftly cut away the rim of dough.

At last Obed said, "When Charlie disappeared, Aunt Violet went into a sickness. She lost more than Charlie."

"What do you mean?"

"They hadn't waited for the wedding, you see."

Daniel paused. "You mean . . .?"

"Yes. She lost their baby, too. Aunt Violet never got over the sorrow and the shame of it, unwed as she was."

"But no one points shame at her. No one even talks about it," Daniel said. To himself he added, not even Ross.

"She points shame at herself," Obed said. "And now she has this terrible hatred and fear of the sea."

The hours of daylight grew longer and the weather sometimes milder, but Obed said they could still expect some of the worst storms of the year. Toward the end of March such a heavy fog set in that the men could see nothing from the watch house and had to patrol during the day as well as at night.

One afternoon Abner failed to return on schedule from the north patrol. Daniel and Will were in the mess polishing brass when the captain came out to ask about Abner.

"Better go look for him, Will," he said.

Daniel jumped up. "Let me go too, Captain. Please!"

"Granted."

Daniel and Will put on their storm gear hastily and set out with lanterns. It was still daylight but the fog remained dense. Foghorns blared mournfully. Daniel and Will hurried along near the surf where the sand was wet and hard. With lanterns to the ground, they looked for boot prints or some other sign of Abner. They shouted for him in vain.

At halfway house they found hot ashes in the stove and two coffee cups, clean but still warm.

"He made it this far and started back," Will said.

"But we didn't see his footprints going either way."

"Oh, Daniel, of course not!" Will dashed out.

Daniel ran after him. "What's the matter?"

"It's spring tide! When Abner was patrolling, the surf must have been up to the dunes. He'd have gone along the top."

Will found a place where he and Daniel could claw their way up the cliff.

Will moaned. "Oh, I can't even keep my mind on something like this! I don't deserve to be a surfman. I should have remembered spring tide."

"I should have, too!" Daniel said.

They tramped over pits, hollows, and mounds, through clumps of drenched beach grass and webbed roots.

"Be careful, Daniel," Will said. "The dunes could give way anywhere."

Swinging their lanterns left and right, they looked for trampled grass. They shouted for Abner but heard only the foghorn, the swishing surf below, the pounding breakers, and their thundering echo under the cliffs. They crossed gullies in the dunes cut by rivulets washing back to sea. Will said this must be the way Abner had come, but still they found no sign of him.

Within half an hour's walk of their station, Daniel thought he heard someone call. Rushing on, Will stopped short, just where the edge of a deep gully was hidden by grass.

"Watch out, Daniel!"

Will found a more gentle slope, and they both slid down to the bank of a stream that was sweeping back to sea.

"There he is!" Daniel cried.

Abner lay at the water's edge, drenched and coated with sand and clay. "My leg!" he gasped.

Will put down his lantern and knelt beside him. Abner had one boot off and had slit the leg of his trousers, his stockings, and his long underwear. Will pulled the clothing aside and exposed a swollen, grotesque lower leg.

"I saw you go toward Pamet." Abner was breathing hard. "I tried to call out. I was afraid you wouldn't find me."

"You're all right now, Abner," Will said. "But we'll have to immobilize your leg before we can get you back to the station. Daniel, please find something—driftwood, anything. Just make sure it's long enough."

Daniel rushed along the stream and out to the beach where the tide had receded. It seemed forever before he turned up a narrow plank under a mass of seaweed. He was able to break the plank off to about the length of Abner's leg.

When he got back he found that Will had wrapped his own jacket around Abner and had torn his own shirt into strips. Abner suppressed groans as Will supported the injured leg with the driftwood and tied it gently in place with the strips.

Daniel helped Will get Abner up and they held him between them. It was slow going on the bank of the rivulet until they reached harder sand.

"Thank you!" Abner said. "Thank you both! I was so worried. What would my wife and my boy ever do without me?" He shuddered, slipped through their hold, and fell.

"He's fainted," Will said. "All the better for him. Here, Daniel, please carry my lantern."

Will picked Abner up and walked with him as nimbly as though he had no burden. With nothing more than two lanterns to carry, Daniel found it hard to keep up.

TWENTY-FOUR

DANIEL THREW OPEN the station door.

"Captain! We found Abner!"

The captain dashed out of his office. Trueheart scrambled down the stairs followed by Jon. Obed appeared from the boat room and Ross from the galley.

"You crazy fool!" Ross yelled at Abner, who was limp in Will's arms. "What did you do to yourself?"

"Crazy fool yourself!" Daniel cried. "Can't you see he's only half conscious!"

"Give him to me," the captain said. "Jon, come help me. You others get out of the way."

The captain carried Abner upstairs. Jon and Trueheart followed. The others stared after them, Daniel and Will still in their clay-smeared boots and slickers.

Jon was soon back. "Abner's come to. His leg is broken and he's got a bad chill. Ross, take him coffee and hot soup, if you got some. Obed, please go for the doctor."

Daniel and Will got out of their gear and went to the galley for coffee.

Staring into his mug, Will said, "I'm not fit to be a surfman any longer. I'll try to finish the season, then I'll go away. There are other things worth doing, work on the newspaper maybe."

Daniel longed to tell Will Rachel's secret and make him happier at once, but he told himself again that he shouldn't do it without her permission.

The doctor arrived in his buggy with Abner's wife, Sarah, leaving Obed to walk back. There seemed to be little more to Sarah than a shawl topped by a bonnet. She looked dazed.

Daniel offered to show the doctor up to the infirmary.

"I know the way," the doctor said. "Been here often enough." He allowed only Sarah to go with him.

She was soon back. "He let me say hello, is all."

Daniel jumped up to take her bonnet and shawl. Will brought her a chair. Ross offered coffee.

"Tea, if it's no trouble." She huddled against the stove, ignoring the tea Ross handed to her. When the doctor came in, she jumped to her feet, tipping over her cup.

The doctor was a spindly man with wispy gray hair, but his voice was that of someone used to giving orders.

"Sit back down there, Sarah. You look worse than Abner." He took her pulse. "Somebody give her another

173

cup of tea. See she drinks it this time. And get me some coffee."

"What about Abner?" Ross asked. For once he was not laughing and he looked like a different man.

The doctor gulped coffee before bothering to answer. "Got a fracture and no mistake. Tibia, above the right ankle. But it could be worse. You fellas did a fair enough job with your makeshift splint, but it was his giant muscles that kept the bone in place. I've put him in proper splints. See he drinks plenty of milk for the calcium."

He looked into his cup with a frown. "Who brewed this stuff? Must have been you, Ross." He held out his cup for more.

"Will he be all right then, Doctor?" Sarah asked.

"Of course. The man's an ox. But he's got a fever. Be in bed a while."

"Then I must take him home," Sarah said.

"No, you must not. He is not to be moved."

"Oh, Doctor, please."

The doctor's old face softened. "Don't you fuss, Sarah. Just go home and tend to yourself and that boy of yours. Your Abner is in good hands right here."

The captain revised the schedule to cover for Abner and assigned most of Abner's care to Daniel, who had to give up church and his day off.

Daniel fretted and worried, impatient to see Rachel about Will, afraid she might give Percy her promise before he could speak to her. However, he did his best for Abner—helped him bathe, carried his food, emptied his slops, stood by for the doctor's visits.

Feverish, Abner talked more than usual, mostly about Sarah and his son, but he thanked Daniel again and again.

"You're a good lad, Daniel. I didn't think so at first. You put me in mind of that Percy Yates."

Daniel was appalled. "Percy Yates!"

"Well, you talked so uppity at first, acting as how you come down in the world here with us. But you proved you're all right. Percy could never do all you done."

The first Sunday Abner's temperature was normal, Daniel got permission to go to church. He set out early and waited at the church door for Rachel and Fannie. To his frustration, Aunt Violet appeared on Rachel's arm. He took Fannie aside.

"Please ask Rachel to see me after service. Can you keep Aunt Violet away? I'll tell you everything later."

After church, Rachel met Daniel with a broad smile. "Just look at you! You've grown like a weed. Your sleeves are up on your arms till it's almost a disgrace."

Daniel hardly thought about clothes these days, but his face went warm at the idea of appearing comical to Rachel. He tried to pull his sleeves down.

"But you look handsome," Rachel added. "Rosy, brown, and muscular. Your mother will be proud of you."

She examined his sleeves. "I'll let the hems down. Give your suit to Father, his next day off."

"That's good of you, Rachel. Very good. Thank you. But there's something else. Important. It's about Will."

The smile left her face. "He's not hurt?"

"No. But he means to quit the service and go work for the newspaper in Provincetown."

"That can't be so. The service is the most important thing in his life."

"No, Rachel. You are. Only you."

She turned away.

"He hasn't guessed it's the service that keeps you apart. He thinks he's offended you and he's suffering because he can't think how."

"Oh, Daniel." Tears glistened in Rachel's eyes.

"Talk to him, Rachel. Please!"

"I shall. But I have something to settle first."

"Percy? He'll be home soon, won't he?"

She did not answer. Daniel said, "I don't mean to pry."

"Never mind. I thank you with all my heart."

TWENTY-FIVE

NOW AT THE BEGINNING of April, the weather was sometimes clear, sometimes cloudy, windy, misty, or rainy, and often cold, even with occasional sleet and hail.

When Abner could care for himself, Daniel begged to patrol in his place, to ease the extra burden the men had assumed while Abner was disabled. To Daniel's surprise, the captain agreed.

Carrying Abner's check to trade with the Pamet River surfman, Daniel patrolled on what was called the sunrise watch, although it was dark most of the time.

Daniel could hardly contain his pride, even though the responsibility made him anxious and the trek was lonely. On his first patrol the cold was severe and he suffered frostbite, but he had nothing to report.

On the third day, the coast was hit by a severe northeaster. Daniel plunged through wind and rain, holding a shingle to his face against cutting blasts of sand. He made it to the halfway house, traded checks and banter with Fortune Smith, and started home more easily, with wind at his back.

About an hour later, the breakers were high and the surf a close, rushing flood. Daniel was thinking of climbing up to walk along the cliff's edge when he heard a boom unlike the thunder of breakers.

He stopped to scan the ocean intently. The boom sounded again and then again. It could only be a ship's cannon. And there was a flicker of fire near the shoals.

Daniel waded out as far as he could without being swept off his feet. He grew certain. Either a vessel was on fire or its seamen were burning something as another signal of distress. They were in desperate trouble.

Daniel had never struck a Coston light, although Obed had shown him how to use them. Could he ignite the thing properly, or would it burn his hand or go off in his face?

Hesitating only a moment, he snatched one of the cylinders from his belt and struck it. A brilliant flare burst forth.

Daniel waved the light. "We're coming! Hold on!"

He knew he could not be heard and he was not sure his signal had been seen, but when the flare fizzled out, he broke into a run back to the station. With the wind at his back, he almost flew off his feet.

Lungs bursting and heart battering his ribs, he crashed through the door to the mess crying, "Vessel in trouble!"

The office door flew open and the captain appeared.

Ed came from the galley. Will and Ross tumbled downstairs pulling on their clothes.

Daniel was elated that the men had responded to his cry. Had he been afraid Ross would sneer?

"Vessel shooting her gun, Captain. Got fire aboard."

"Where is she?"

"About a mile north. On the shoals, I think."

"We're going out!" the captain cried.

The men dashed for the boat room. Abner came limping down the steps. "What is it, Captain?"

"Nothing for you, Number Four! Get back to bed."

Daniel started for the boat room, but the captain said, "Stay here, Daniel. You're exhausted and drenched. Make coffee. We're going to need plenty."

"But you're short-handed, sir. Jon's still on patrol. Obed's on leave. Who's going to help launch the boat? Who's going to keep the lanterns going and build a fire on the beach?"

"Haven't I told you not to dispute my orders?"

"I can make the coffee, sir," Abner said.

"Please let me go with you, Captain," Daniel begged. "I'm not tired. I can help. You need me!"

The captain scowled, then relented. "Come on, then!"

Daniel was amazed at how fast the men dressed in boots and slickers and got the boat carriage down to the beach. Though short-handed, the men seemed to work faster than in any drill. But it was a grueling struggle to pull the boat over the sand against the shrieking wind.

By the time they reached the scene, the sky was light

179

at the horizon, but the breakers were still roaring and the surf was wild. Now Daniel could see the rigging of the vessel as she rocked furiously against the sky. Her cannon was silent and the fire gone.

The men pushed the carriage to the surf and got the boat dismounted.

"See anybody aboard, Captain?" Ed shouted as the men got into their life belts.

"It's still too dark."

"She's taking a pounding on those shoals," Ross said. "She can't last much longer."

The men took their places at the gunwales. Daniel stood at the stern with the captain, watching the waves roll in, waiting for the slatch.

"Send up a flare, Daniel!" the captain cried. "Start a fire under the dunes. Keep the lanterns lit."

"Yes, sir! I know what to do."

"Now!" the captain cried.

The men rushed the boat out on the receding surf and leaped aboard. Daniel splashed out with them. Drenched to the neck, he held the stern, fighting with the plunging boat to keep it from going broadside while the captain jumped in.

A gigantic wave crashed against the boat. Daniel was thrown to his knees in the surf. The stern was wrenched out of his hands. The boat turned sideways. Another wave crashed over it. The boat went spinning, bounced up on one side, and threw the men into the sea.

Daniel struggled to his feet. His sou'wester tore off

his head. The captain, Ross, and Ed got the surfboat in hand and wrestled it to shore.

"Daniel, look for Will!" the captain shouted.

For a horrible moment while he scanned the waves Daniel thought of Aunt Violet. Would the sea do their family another wrong?

But there was Will's face, just above water. He looked dazed, down in the surf in the path of another breaker. Daniel struggled out and reached him as the wave crashed over them both. He got Will to his feet, and together they stumbled to the beach. Will's right arm was dangling.

The captain hurried over.

Will was laughing oddly. "The boat slammed into me, knocked me flat. For a minute I thought I was dreaming."

Daniel supported Will in the buffeting wind while the captain helped him out of his life belt and examined his shoulder. "Afraid it's your collarbone, son."

Edwin called, "No damage to the boat, Captain. We can take her out again."

Will's laugh had grown shrill. "Thought sure I'd stoved her in." He picked up his life belt and started for the boat.

"Where do you think you're going?" the captain cried.

"You won't make it without me, not in a storm like this."

"Didn't you hear me? Your collarbone is broken."

"I can row with one arm, Captain!"

"You're off your head!" Ross cried.

"He's in shock, Captain," Ed said. He turned to Will. "Listen, son. You don't feel it yet, but you'll soon be helpless. You'd be a handicap in the boat."

The captain said, "Daniel, take him back and then go for the doctor. Ask someone at the church to ring for the villagers."

"I'll go back myself," Will said. "Jon can go to the village when he comes off patrol. You need Daniel here." He walked away sturdily along the beach.

"He'll be all right, sir," Edwin said.

Ross went back to the boat. "We can get her out now!"

"Make ready to launch!" the captain called.

The men nosed the boat into the surf. Daniel stepped into Will's place at the midship oar.

"Get out of there!" the captain shouted.

"You need my oar, Captain!" Daniel cried.

"He's right, sir," Ed said. "I doubt we can get back without another oar."

"We have to go out," the captain said. "We don't have to come back."

"We'll come back and the seamen with us, if you let me row!" Daniel cried.

"He can do it, Captain," Edwin said.

Ross shouted at Daniel, "Get into a life belt, you fool!"

TWENTY-SIX

THIS WAS NO MERE DRILL but real action at last. Daniel was elated to be taking Will's place at the starboard midship oar, lined up with these mighty surfmen, Ross at the harpooner's oar, Ed at the stroke. Even in this black weather, wind, and raging sea, Daniel had no fear. He was eager for the captain's order.

"Launch!"

The men rushed the boat into the surf. Ross leaped aboard. Daniel clambered in next and wrestled his oar into its lock. Ed jumped in and then the captain.

"Pull!" the captain roared. "Pull for your life!"

The captain was a giant, upright in the stern, wind whipping his slickers and spray crashing over him, his powerful arms holding the steering oar steady and the boat head-on into the breakers. Even Daniel's mother, who so admired her brother, could not know what a hero he was.

But Daniel had no time to dwell on it. A great sea washed over the bow onto his back, shocking him. The boat shuddered stem to stern but the men did not miss a stroke. Deluged again and again, they pulled on. Water sloshed in the bottom of the boat.

"Bail, Daniel!" the captain roared.

Daniel fumbled for the bucket. Scooping water, still keeping a grip on his oar, he tried to ignore the spray cutting his face, the salt stinging his nose and lips.

By now the sun was up under rolling clouds. Wind whipped the sea and whistled around the boat. Daniel lost track of how long he pulled, straining to keep in rhythm with Ed and Ross. His hands were numb, the seat of his pants was soaked, and the rough cloth chafed his skin.

He was roused from a stupor of rowing by the sound of moaning, cracking timbers.

"She's breaking up!" Ross cried.

Daniel snatched a look over his shoulder. The vessel lay dead ahead, bow to the east and stern toward shore. Her forestaysail and jib were blowing in rags. Her mainsail was standing full, the mainsheet half out. Her boom was slapping the sea as she rolled to leeward and pulling up as she rolled back. A noise like gunshots rang out above the storm.

Daniel turned for another look and saw that the popping came from sails slatting in the wind. A fat man was hanging over the stern with two young seamen and a boy of about twelve.

The fat man waved frantically. "Help us! Hurry, hurry!"

Another seaman shouted through cupped hands. "Have a care for the boom, sir! Keep to our stern!"

Until this moment, Daniel had thought of what he and the surfmen were doing as a challenge to their mettle, a great adventure. Now he went icy with horror. These terrified living people, with families and friends who loved them, would die in the sea unless Daniel and the surfmen could save them.

"Put your backs to it!" the captain cried. "We'll go up under her stern."

The men rowed closer to the rocking, groaning vessel.

"You men aboard!" the captain called. "Stand by for a line."

Ross threw the bowline. One of the young seamen caught it and made it fast.

"Ross, pull us in," the captain ordered.

Ross hauled on the bowline.

"Daniel, hold off with the boat hook. Don't let us get swept under the counter."

Daniel snatched the boat hook and shoved its tip against the sloop to steady the bounding surfboat.

"Come aboard!" the captain shouted to the seamen.

The fat man hoisted a kit onto the sloop's rail.

"No baggage!" the captain roared.

"I need this! It's my best clothes!" The man aimed his kit at the surfboat. It fell on Daniel's lap.

"Toss it overboard!" the captain cried.

The fat man howled. "Don't you dare!"

"Toss it!"

Daniel heaved the kit into the sea. It rode on the waves, took water, and sank.

The fat man pounded the rail. "You bastard!"

"None of that!" the captain shouted. "We're here to save your life, not your goods."

"At the risk of our own, you damn fool!" Ross yelled.

"None of that from you, either, Ross," the captain said. He called, "You seamen, get in our boat. The boy first."

The fat man shoved the boy aside, climbed over the rail of the sloop, and tumbled into the surfboat, sending it rocking and shipping water.

"Why, you son of a—" Ross yelled.

"Lie down," the captain ordered the seaman.

"But there's bilge—" the man protested.

"Get down, I say! Ross, flatten him."

Ross shoved the man down.

"Ugh! You got me all wet."

Ross yelled in his face, "You'll be a damn sight wetter if you make us capsize!"

"You seamen, hand the boy down to us," the captain called. The young seamen lowered the boy and climbed down after him.

"Ross, cut the bowline," the captain ordered.

"Wait, wait!" the boy screamed. "My father!"

A bearded man in a visored cap appeared at the rail.

"Skipper?" the captain called.

"Aye!"

"Get in, sir. There's room for all."

"I'm not leaving." The skipper stood at the rail, the wind flapping his pea jacket.

"Do you mean to go down with your sloop? She's breaking up, sir!"

The men shouted at each other above the screaming wind and the creaking, groaning vessel.

"She's not. I know my sloop. She's weathered worse."

"You've not had her on these shoals before, I'll wager. Get in, sir, I beg you!"

"I'll not."

"Then tell me who you are!"

"Roger Bowls. This is the *Sarah Lee Watkins* of Rockport, bound for home port from New Bedford."

"Any cargo?"

"Twenty tons of coal for ballast."

"Anyone else aboard?"

"No one."

"For the last time, sir, please!"

"Take my men. I don't ask them to stay, but this is my own vessel and I don't mean to lose her."

The skipper untied the bowline and cast it into the surfboat.

The boy flew up. "I'll stay with you, Father!"

"No, Alex!" the skipper called. "Hold him down, somebody."

Daniel pushed the boy to the bottom of the surfboat.

"So be it!" the captain cried. "Don't try to come ashore in your sloop's boat, except as a last resort. You'll find it hard to judge this sea."

The boy sobbed. "Oh, Father, come with us! Please!"

"Go along, son. Look after your mother."

"Shove off!" the captain ordered.

Daniel pushed the surfboat away from the sloop with the boat hook and took his oar.

One of the young seamen said, "Can we help you row, sir?"

"No, thanks," the captain said. "My men are trained for this."

Daniel swelled with pride, but he did not feel complacent. With the men safe off their vessel the important part of their job was done, but he knew that pulling to shore with powerful waves astern was extremely hazardous. Great skill and strength were needed at the oars, especially the steering oar, to keep the sea from overtaking the boat, tossing it end over end, or turning it broadside and making it capsize.

"We'll keep her head to the sea," the captain said. "We'll go in stern foremost."

Daniel had practiced this maneuver with the crew. On command, the men pulled a few strokes back into each oncoming wave until it passed, and then resumed rowing stern first to shore. Even backward, the boat flew.

The boy lay moaning in bilge.

"Don't worry, son," Daniel said, gasping between hard pulls on his oar. He had never felt so manly or so proud of what he was doing. "Our captain is the best."

"But sir, what about my father?"

Ross said, "Pray for him." Daniel was surprised to hear no sarcasm in that, no sneering or joking. For once, Ross sounded sincere.

They pulled on. The boy grew quiet and the two young seamen said nothing, but the fat man whimpered. "I'm freezing. I'm sick. I'm going to throw up."

Ross bellowed at him, "Shut your mouth, you coward!"

Daniel was rowing with all his strength, cold to the bone, aching in every muscle. He tried to think of nothing but hot soup, dry clothes, and his own warm bed.

He became aware of church bells and of firelight glittering on the beach.

"The villagers are here, thank God," Edwin said.

They reached the shallows. Men from the village ran into the surf to help. The young seamen and the boy jumped out with the crew to pull the boat ashore, but the fat man stayed aboard until the boat was up on the sand. He trotted straight for the bonfires built under the embankment.

A seaman roared at him, "Cookie, you blackguard!" The seaman turned to the captain and touched his cap. "Levi Benson, first mate. I thank you for all, sir."

"No need for that, Benson. It's just our job."

To the men and women from the village crowding around, the captain said, "Would some of you folks please get these men to the station?"

"Aren't you coming, sir?" the first mate asked.

"We're going out again," Daniel's uncle said. "I think your skipper will see reason by now."

The boy burst into sobs. "Oh, thank you, sir!"

Daniel was shocked. He ached all over, his ears were ringing, he was dizzy, soaked, and frozen. So must be the captain, Ed, and Ross, he thought.

"Daniel, go back with the others," his uncle said. "You've done enough."

When Ross grinned, Daniel flared with anger. Daniel had done as well as any of them, no one could deny it.

"No, sir! Excuse me, sir. It's not enough till the job is done."

"Good man!" Ed said.

Two husky villagers stepped forward. One said, "Captain, we'll go out with you."

The captain looked hard at Daniel, then turned to the volunteers, "No, thanks. I need my trained men for this. Just stand by, please, and keep the fires going. Crew, prepare to launch!"

TWENTY-SEVEN

DANIEL AND THE SURFMEN rushed the boat out again. Daniel pulled his oar as heartily as he could, teeth clenched, eyes closed. He lost any concept of time until, once more, he was roused by the slatting of sails.

Now the sloop's quarter was toward them. The vessel was lower in the sea, rocking with a great crunching of timbers. Her mainsail was standing full, the tip of her boom still slapping water as she rolled.

"What a pity," Edwin muttered. "She's a beauty."

"Was a beauty," Ross said. "She's done for."

"Pull in closer," the captain ordered.

But the surfboat was swept back by a sea.

"Pull up again!"

They rowed toward the vessel once more.

The captain called, "Hello, aboard!"

The sloop's skipper came to the rail.

"Your ship is going down, sir. You must come with us! Stand by for our line."

Ross stood up in the bow ready to heave the line.

"Daniel, hold off with the boat hook," the captain cried. "Skipper! Make fast our line, I say!"

The skipper did not move. "This is my vessel. I'm master here. I'll not take orders from you!"

The sloop rolled to leeward.

"Watch out for the boom!" Ed shouted.

A sea came around the stern and threw the surfboat toward the boom as it came down. The sloop rolled to windward. The boom went up again, catching the gunwale of the surfboat. The surfboat flew over.

Daniel was under black, icy water. He struggled to the surface. Salt stung his nose and eyes. He bobbed on the waves, buoyed by his life belt, but the sea kept breaking over his face. Oars, boat hook, lines, gear, and wreckage tumbled around him. He saw the surfboat bounding on the waves to his left, right side up but empty.

The boom swooped down again and crashed over the surfboat. With a great sound of splintering, the sloop's mast cracked. The boom broke loose and smacked the sea in a tangle of rigging and canvas.

Choking, floundering in the waves, Daniel cast about wildly. "Captain, Captain!"

He saw a man in the tangle of rigging among timbers, ropes, and canvas churning in the sea. The man went under, came up again. Blood streaked his forehead, washed away, and spurted again through his hair.

Daniel cried, "Oh, Uncle Elisha!"

Coughing, the man called weakly, "Daniel!"

Daniel saw the man's beard. So, it was not his uncle!

"Ross!" In relief, and as resentful of Ross as ever, Daniel rejoiced. So it's Daniel, now! he thought. No more Six and a Half. He wanted to laugh.

Jon had said earth had the right to take life. If it took Ross, it was no fault of Daniel's. Why should he care?

Ross called, "Daniel, stay clear! Don't get caught in this. Don't try to save me, surfman."

The sea closed over Ross's head.

Daniel was flooded with shame. If he knew anything about the surfmen by now, it was that they did what they could, no matter what, no matter for whom. Fearful but determined, he thrashed toward Ross. A broken timber drove at Daniel's head. He threw up his arms, diverted it, pushed on.

Shoving aside ropes and beams, he fought to get his head clear for a gulp of air and then dived. Underwater, struggling against the pull of his life belt, he could see nothing, but groping, found Ross's head and grabbed him by the hair. He could not get him up. Crawling down by holds on Ross's slickers, he found Ross's legs snarled in rope.

Ross slipped through Daniel's hands. Daniel's life belt dragged him to the surface. Again he swept the sea with his hands, caught Ross's clothes, and pulled himself under. He got out his knife and sawed at the tangle of ropes. It seemed minutes before a rope parted. He sawed at another rope and another. His lungs were bursting. Bubbles escaped from his mouth. He went faint.

The knife dropped from his hand. He could not tell which way was up, but something dragged him. He exploded into air.

Choking, deafened by water in his ears, lungs aflame, Daniel looked about for Ross. Ross, too, was on the surface, floating in his life belt, his face white as a fish. Blood pumped through his hair and down his beard.

Daniel tore off a strip of his shirt and bound Ross's head. The bandage went red with blood.

Holding Ross's face above the sea, Daniel pulled him clear of the ropes and wreckage.

He glanced about desperately. "Captain! Ed!"

The sloop was lower in the sea now and rocking feebly. The surfboat had moved off, broken but afloat.

Daniel's urgent thought was to get away from the sinking sloop or be pulled down after it. Dragging Ross, he swam to the surfboat. It was a struggle to shove the heavy, limp Ross out of the water, but he got him up at last across the gunwale and rolled him into the boat. Slipping and trying again, he finally got in himself. The wrecked surfboat was very low in the water, but it did not go down.

"Good old boat!" Daniel cried, with a rush of love.

Daniel looked about at the wreckage tumbling in the waves and at last saw an oar. He nearly upset the boat before he caught it. With the oar he managed to maneuver farther away from the sinking sloop.

He shouted again, "Captain! Ed!"

"Daniel!" It was Ed, calling from beyond the wreck. Daniel heard his uncle. "You all right, son?"

"Yes, sir! Ross is here, too, but he's bleeding. We have the surfboat. We'll come for you."

"No! The boat's broken. It won't take us all. Get it away from here. The sloop will go down any minute."

"No, sir! No, sir!"

"Get away, I tell you! Go in with the rollers. Don't fight them. The sea is calmer now. You can make it."

"Not without you!"

"We've got the mast. We'll get back on that when we find the sloop's master. We'll be all right."

Daniel burst into sobs. "Please don't make me leave you."

"Go back, I say! Get help for Ross. That's an order."

Sobbing, Daniel turned the boat. He struggled with the oar, trying to keep the boat in control, but it spun, tossed, and turned, swept along by the waves.

"We'll get there, Ross. The captain is always right."

Ross kept rolling from side to side, causing the boat to ship water. It seemed a lot of time passed without much progress as Daniel tried to steady Ross with his feet while he worked the oar.

A wave washed into the boat. Ross rolled over the side into the sea. Daniel tried to snag him with the oar. The oar slipped out of his hands. Daniel went into the water, caught Ross, and wrestled him back into the boat. The boat was now so low in the waves that Daniel did not dare get back in himself.

He held onto the side and, with his strong swimmer's kick, tried to keep the boat's nose to shore as it passed in surges from one roller to the next.

The sun was higher now, behind ruby-edged clouds. At last Daniel saw the bonfires on the beach and his hopes rose.

"We're almost there, Ross! We'll get you help."

But the dreadful breakers were ahead. Daniel felt them take powerful hold of the broken surfboat. The boat went flying, turning and bouncing, but instead of nearing the beach, it rushed alongshore in the undertow.

Bonfires and dunes pulled away. Sea and clouds went spinning. The gunwales were so low in the water that Ross was nearly over them again. Swimming as close to the boat as he could, Daniel kept one frozen hand clamped to the gunwale and the other on Ross.

A sea broke over Daniel's head. Something slipped past him. It was Ross, sweeping away, bobbing in his life belt. Daniel pushed off from the boat, swam after him, and caught him by the hair. The boat spun out of reach.

Buoyed by the life belts, Daniel managed to clamp Ross in a cross-chest hold. He swam with all the strength he had, pulling with his other arm and kicking, trying to make for the beach, but the undertow was strong. The bonfires slipped farther away.

Daniel began to despair. Soon he hardly knew whether he was conscious or not. As in a dream he thought he saw shadowy figures running along the shore, thought he heard men shouting, a seal barking.

Something came pushing toward Daniel through the breaking waves, black nose and eyes just above the water.

"Trueheart!" Daniel cried.

The dog's massive body nudged him. Her great jaws clamped on a strap of Ross's life belt. Her powerful legs and huge paws struck out for shore. Swimming together, dragging Ross between them, they got past the undertow.

Men came rushing at them through the surf. Someone hauled Daniel to his feet, but he slipped. The beach flew up and slammed against his knees and clawed his face.

TWENTY-EIGHT

DANIEL WAS IN THE SURFBOAT, dragging his oar, his
shoulders alive with pain. No, he was in the sea, rolling
in the breakers. He was shaking with cold, yet he knew
he was warm and dry. He opened his eyes and found
himself in bed in the infirmary. Somebody's big hands
were tumbling his head in a towel. He pushed free and
saw Obed.

Daylight was streaming through the windows. A man
with stringy hair and a stain on his tie bent over him,
holding one end of a wooden tube to Daniel's chest
while he kept his ear to the other. He tossed the instrument into a scruffy satchel and pinched Daniel's wrist
between bony fingers.

When Daniel opened his eyes again he saw someone
under covers on a cot at the far end of the room. The
doctor was still holding Daniel's wrist. Obed was there,
too, with a towel looped between his big hands.

Daniel was about to complain that his ears were ringing, but the doctor slipped a thermometer under his tongue.

"You look better, Danny!" Obed said. "Lucky Doc was here to set Will's collarbone and tend those seamen. Doc says they all ought to be abed same as you, but they're still eating, especially that fat man. There's a boy keeps crying."

"Obed, I thought you were on leave," Daniel said.

"I come back with the villagers when we heard the church bells."

"Obed, leave off your jawing and give this young fella whatever you got as a restorative," the doctor said. "Might as well use what the government pays for and save mine."

Obed went to the medicine cupboard and returned with a bottle and spoon. The doctor took the thermometer out of Daniel's mouth, held it to the light, shook it down, wiped it, and stowed it in his breast pocket.

"I'm wasting my time on you."

"How is Ross, Doctor?" Daniel asked. "Did you see the gash on his head? It was bleeding a lot."

"Take your medicine," the doctor said.

Obed poured liquid into the spoon and held it out. The heavy liquid was stronger than anything Daniel had ever tasted. Flame shot up his nose and scalded his throat.

The doctor nodded. "Now lie back and let it work."

"Ross?" Daniel asked again.

"Don't worry about a thing." The doctor closed the snaps on his satchel. "Obed, any coffee left?"

"Sure, Doc, we got plenty. We always got plenty."

The doctor started for the door. "Who made the stuff? Wasn't you, was it? Not up to your standard."

"Doc, you always find fault with our coffee but you never turn it down."

The doctor went out grumbling. "I take it as restorative. I'm near dead. Up half the night with the depot master's eldest and then your man come pounding on my door."

"If you need anything, give a holler." Obed turned to follow the doctor.

"Wait! Did the captain and Ed get back all right?"

"You heard the doctor. Rest. Don't talk."

Daniel could not worry for long. Warm, comforting sleep took him away.

When he awoke, he saw that the seamen and the boy had all been put to bed in the other cots in the infirmary. Feeling befuddled but ravenous, Daniel got dressed. He thought the mess below did not sound the same as usual. Instead of brassy tones and huge laughter, there was a hum of quiet voices. He went down.

Benches had been set up around the walls and people were sitting everywhere, giving the place the look of a depot waiting room. Some were strangers, some were people he knew. Obed's grandmother was there, knitting. Abner's wife had her head on his shoulder, their son asleep on the bench beside them. Fannie leaned back, eyes closed.

Rachel was with Will, who had one arm around her and the other in a sling. They were talking quietly, eye to eye. Daniel was elated to see them looking so intimate. Obviously, all was now right between them.

Ross's wife was sitting between her two sons. She jumped up and took Daniel's hands. Her usually jolly face was pale and strained. The boys looked on blankly.

"Daniel, how are you?"

"Fine, Mrs. Ogilvie. But stupid from the medicine they gave me."

"You haven't taken a chill?"

"No, ma'am. Doc said he was wasting his time on me."

Her smile seemed made with an effort. "We're just waiting for Wilbur to come with his cart and help us take Ross home. Thank you, Daniel, for bringing him back to us. I'll never forget your courage."

Daniel repeated with pride what his uncle had said to the seaman on the beach. "No need for thanks. It's our job."

To his surprise, Mrs. Ogilvie kissed him, then turned away to press a handkerchief to her face.

"Can I bring you and the boys something to eat?"

"No thank you, dear Daniel."

Daniel made Obed's grandmother the same offer, but she, too, declined. He went to the mess table to see what he could find for himself, but there were only empty dishes.

Obed called from the galley, "I'll fix you something."

Daniel sat at the worktable while Obed scrambled eggs.

"What's everybody doing here?" Daniel asked.

"Waiting for news of Ed, the captain, and the skipper."

"They're not back?" Daniel jumped up.

Obed barred his way. "Where do you think you're going?"

"To get my slickers."

"No, you ain't. You can't do no good. The Pamet crew's gone out. Jon, Trueheart, the superintendent, and the villagers are searching from here to Peaked Hill Bars. They'll find them, never fear."

Obed sat him down again. "Best you eat something."

Obed brought his skillet to the table. Daniel thought he had lost his appetite, but when Obed served the eggs, he changed his mind. Obed stood beside him, slicing bread.

Daniel asked, "Why is Ross going home? Is he hurt bad?"

Obed's knife stopped. "Danny, don't you know?"

Daniel felt a creeping dread. "Know what, Obed?"

"Oh, Danny, I'm sorry. Ross. You see, Ross, he . . ." Obed's face twitched. "It won't be the same here without him. He kept us so lively, always jolly, always funning." Tears ran down Obed's plump cheeks. He dropped the bread knife and put his fists to his eyes.

"No, Obed. That can't be. We came back together in the surfboat. Then Trueheart and I brought him in."

"Danny, listen. I feel so bad to tell you, but Doc said he was dead before you got him ashore."

"No! I don't believe it. Where is he?"

"He's covered over, in the infirmary."

"I want to see him!"

"You should be still abed." Obed pushed Daniel back into his chair. He brought a glass of water. "Drink this."

Daniel could not swallow. "He told me not to save him, Obed. He was afraid for me. For me! Oh, God forgive me!"

When Obed thumped him on the back, Daniel realized he was sobbing.

"You mustn't feel any blame, Danny. You did all you could. You had to try. He didn't have to live."

"But I never told him that I'm sorry."

"Sorry? Nobody could have done better."

"Not that. Sorry that I hated him." Daniel buried his face in his arms. "He called me surfman!"

When he could calm himself, Daniel went back to the mess. Obed followed and stood watching as Daniel spoke to Ross's wife. "Mrs. Ogilvie, I didn't realize. You see, I thought—oh, I can't believe it!"

"Never mind, Daniel. You mustn't grieve. It's something a surfman's family is always prepared for."

To Obed, she said, "Will you pray for us?"

"But I'm not in command. It's Number Four, just now. That's you, Abner."

"You're the one for it, Obed."

Obed's grandmother nodded. "Yes, Obed. You're the one."

There was a murmur of assent. Obed knelt and everyone around the room followed suit. Obed was quiet so long that Daniel peered at him and saw his head bowed, his big hands covering his face.

When Obed spoke at last, it was as though to someone among them. "Father, we pray for the soul of Ross, our dear comrade, and for Adah and her children that they may be comforted. We pray for Daniel who was ready to lay down his life for our friend. May Daniel remember what our Lord said, that no man could show greater love."

Daniel choked back his tears.

Obed went on. "We pray for Ed and our captain and the master of the sloop, that they may come back to us safely."

Obed fell silent while everyone waited. Finally he said, "Thy will be done."

"Thy will be done," said everyone.

Obed remained on his knees. At last he said, "Amen."

When Obed arose, Daniel was surprised to see how joyful he looked.

Before the sun had set behind the dunes, Wilbur took Ross home in his cart, with Adah and her boys. Daniel was sitting with Will, Rachel, and Fannie when the door burst open and Trueheart bounded in, followed by Jon. The dog ran to Daniel, her great black tail thrashing. He threw his arms around her.

"Good girl! Good, brave dog!" He was crying again as she swept her warm tongue over his face.

"Pamet found them, all three," Jon said. "They'll be back in the morning."

TWENTY-NINE

THE DISTRICT SUPERINTENDENT asked if the captain wanted a replacement for Ross to finish the season. The captain said he was proud of the crew he had and they were all he needed.

April slipped away and Daniel's last full day came suddenly. He got leave to go to Fleetport, where he bought tea napkins for his mother and Mrs. O'Till and a book on navigation for Arthur.

Obed's grandmother gave him his choice of duck decoys.

Rachel hugged him. "Good-bye, dear Dan. Will and I have so much to thank you for."

Fannie pumped his hand. "You'll be back in June?"

"For the wedding? I wouldn't miss it."

The next morning Daniel packed his Gladstone and stowed his purchases and his gear in the sea chest, which the captain said he could keep. The captain offered to have Wilbur and Charity take his baggage to the depot, but Daniel said, "Why, Captain, this is nothing."

Ed and Will pounded his back. Obed gave him a great bundle of food for the train. Trueheart brushed around him, staring into his face and wagging feebly, as though she understood it was good-bye.

To Jon, Daniel said, "What you told me when we were on patrol helped me a lot at a bad time, sir."

Jon gave him one of his rare smiles. "We'll all miss you, Daniel."

Abner clamped his hands on Daniel's shoulders. "I'll never forget all you done for me and especially for Ross."

Daniel said, "I know how you feel, sir. I feel the same. You can hate to lose someone, even if you didn't like him much. You can even be sorry you didn't like him."

"You mean me and Ross? Why, that scoundrel was my best friend ever since school. His wife is my cousin."

"Oh, I thought—well, you were always . . ."

"Feuding? Certain we was. Who better to feud with?"

"That's right!" Daniel said. "Ross and I were always feuding, too." He felt relieved of a burden of pain.

Daniel swung the sea chest to his shoulder, picked up his Gladstone, and he and the captain set out together. Even with his baggage, Daniel found it an easy walk to town.

They shipped Daniel's baggage ahead and went out

to the platform. Men touched their caps to the captain. Women nodded to him and also to Daniel, smiling. Daniel glowed with pride. His uncle was a mighty figure of a man, with character to match—brave, steadfast, and honorable. Fair, wise, and strict. Just as he should be.

A smoke cloud rose in the distance. The train appeared, shrieking. Huffing, nosing its cowcatcher along the tracks, the engine ground to a stop, hissing steam.

Boys ran ahead to see the bell-shaped smokestack and the big and bigger wheels. Idlers stepped back and travelers stepped forward.

Here was the moment Daniel had waited for eagerly at first but had now come to dread. He would return, of course, but as a visitor, never again as a surfman.

The captain smiled but Daniel thought he seemed forlorn. Perhaps he had come to like having Daniel there. Daniel and his mother were the captain's only family.

Daniel held out his hand. "Good-bye, Captain."

The captain laughed. "I'm not your captain any longer. You're dismissed."

Daniel flew at him and gave him a hug. "Good-bye, Uncle Elisha. I'll never forget that I served on your crew."

"Nor shall I, Daniel." His uncle took a little case from his breast pocket. "I want you to have this, not just because you're like the son I always wanted; you deserve it."

Daniel knew what was in the box before he opened it. Studying the medal, running his finger over the gleaming surface, he had to wait a long moment before he could say thanks.

On the train, Daniel sank into a stupor, woke, and ate the good lunch Obed had packed for him. With the sandwiches and pie he found a note in a childish hand. "Good-bye to our dear Danny. We miss you."

Later, in the parlor with his mother and Mrs. O'Till, Daniel sat to tea with the new napkins, which they said were remarkable.

He said what he had prepared. "You probably never expected to hear this, but I'm glad you sent me to the lifesavers. It made me grow up."

"So we see," Mrs. O'Till said. "You've lost your fair complexion. And you've gotten so big we'll have to put you into all new clothes."

"Better yet, I'm ahead in all my studies. I expect my masters will be astonished."

"Good for you, my dear son," his mother said.

"And I've been giving serious thought to my future. I'm not sure I want to go into Father's business. Maybe I'll follow in Uncle Elisha's footsteps. Or become a journalist. Or a doctor, like Arthur. Something worthwhile for humanity."

His mother and Mrs. O'Till were smiling constantly.

"By the way, I have to go back in June for a wedding."

"Not your own, I hope!" Mrs. O'Till exclaimed. "Surely you're not that grown up."

Daniel smiled at her tolerantly. "As best man."

His mother nodded. "That's quite grown up enough, for the time being."

They were teasing him, of course, as though he were still the boy they had known. Daniel did not mind. It took a while both to change and to be seen as changed. He would have to let them find it out, little by little.

THE UNITED STATES
LIFE-SAVING SERVICE

THE COASTLINE OF THE UNITED STATES is longer than that of any other nation, and it is extremely dangerous. Before the institution of the United States Life-Saving Service thousands of ships and innumerable lives were lost on its reefs and sandbars. Survival from a shipwreck on the coast was rare.

The shores of Cape Cod, on the "back side," extend along the Atlantic Ocean for some fifty miles, bordered by ever-shifting sandbars, which are a terrible hazard to vessels of every sort. So many ships and lives were lost from the time settlers landed in Provincetown in 1620 that the area came to be known as "Ocean Graveyard." Bodies that washed ashore were buried in unmarked graves in villages all along the coast.

The first organization in the United States to try to provide assistance to shipwreck victims was the Massachusetts Humane Society, now considered the forerunner of the United States Life-Saving Service.

In 1789, on a barren stretch of Lovell's Island, near Boston, the society built a hut to shelter victims who made it to shore. Other shelters followed, and in 1807, at Cohasset, Boston Harbor, the society built the first lifeboat station, manned by volunteers. By 1845, besides refuge huts, the society had established eighteen stations on the Massachusetts coast with lifeboats and rescue equipment. Although the society relied entirely on volunteers for rescue operations, the saving of lives and property was significant.

When the government assumed responsibility a few years later, rescue operations, still with volunteer crews, declined. Loss of life in shipwrecks on the coast was again dreadful. During the winter of 1870–71, so many fatal disasters occurred on the Atlantic Coast that Congress authorized the appointment of paid and trained crews of surfmen at all stations.

Sumner I. Kimball, then head of the Revenue Marine Service and in charge of existing volunteer lifesaving stations, sent one of his officers to study conditions at the stations. The report was appalling—stations filthy and in ruins, equipment in disrepair or stolen, undisciplined crews, and money appropriated for the cause gone to waste.

The need for total reorganization was apparent. In 1872, President Ulysses S. Grant appointed Kimball as General Superintendent of the Life-Saving Service. At first it remained part of the Revenue Marine Service but soon became a separate organization, as the United

States Life-Saving Service, with headquarters in Washington, D.C.

With great dedication and remarkable attention to detail, Kimball organized districts on the Atlantic Coast as well as on lake shores. He had experienced superintendents appointed, along with captains, or keepers, as they were also called, who enlisted the most capable and reliable crews that could be found. The duties of the superintendents heading the twelve districts were many, including overseeing all stations, men, equipment, and operations.

Since some existing stations were too far apart for crews to assist one another in case of need, Kimball authorized the moving of some stations and the construction of others so that no two were more than five miles apart. Rigid discipline and training were established, with regular patrols at night and during the day when weather was too bad for visibility from watch houses. The crew served from September 1 till April 30; the keeper lived at the station and served year round, with volunteers as needed in summer.

The strictly ordered life of surfmen at the stations, their living conditions, organization, regulations, drills, patrols, equipment, and methods of rescue by breeches buoy and surfboat, were just as described in this novel. Some, but not all, of the stations had horses to pull equipment to rescue scenes.

At the outset, surfmen received only $40 a month and keepers $200 a year, but pay was raised later. At first the surfmen had no uniforms, pensions, or insurance to cover injuries. No provision was made for widows and orphans of men killed in the line of duty. Later, Sumner Kimball did get compensation for surfmen who were injured or became ill while on duty, and for widows and orphans, but he never got pensions for retired surfmen.

From the outset, Kimball's organization was spectacularly successful at saving lives from shipwrecks. During the first year, not a life was lost in shipwrecks that occurred on the shores.

Between 1871 and 1888 Kimball reported the number of disasters on the coasts as 4,924, with 42,864 people involved, of whom all but 505 were saved. Before the Life-Saving Service was established, almost everyone would have perished. Sadly, however, throughout the history of the Life-Saving Service, there were valiant surfmen who lost their own lives in the effort to save others.

The Life-Saving Service remained in operation until 1915, when it was united with the Revenue Cutter Service under the name of the United States Coast Guard, as a branch of the armed forces. Members of the Coast Guard received the same pay as men in the navy and wore the same uniforms, with the addition of the Coast Guard insignia.

Duties of the Coast Guard included service at lifeboat stations and on rescue vessels and were greatly expanded to cover enforcing Federal laws at sea and regulations for the safety of life and property at sea — internal revenue, customs, immigration, fisheries and wildlife, security of ports and vessels, and duty in wartime. In the early 1960s, lighthouses also came under Coast Guard jurisdiction. The Coast Guard carries on the old lifesavers' proud tradition of service to country and to humanity, no matter how hazardous the conditions.

ABOUT THE AUTHOR

DONNA HILL WAS A PROFESSOR at Hunter College, City University of New York, and head of the Education Library. She has written fiction and biography for adults as well as fiction and picture books for young people.

In preparation for writing *Shipwreck Season*, Ms. Hill performed extensive research on the history of lifesaving in New England. The nineteenth-century prototype of the lifesavers' station in *Shipwreck Season* is still standing in Wellfleet, Massachusetts (prototype of Fleetport). It is now in use as a restaurant and night-club.

Donna Hill is a life member of the Wellfleet Historical Society and a past president of the New York City Chapter of The Delta Kappa Gamma Society International, honorary organization of educators.